The Tournament

by Kenneth Kirkeby

Printed in the United States of America

ISBN 0-9651410-0-4

Sharp Printing
3477 Lockport Road
Sanborn, NY 14132

CHAPTER I

1978

Ulis told me I had heart. It wasn't what I wanted at the time. It sounded like one of those flying accolades I'd learned to duck when I saw coming. I didn't trust praise. It wouldn't let you any closer to what you wanted. It never got you anything back.

It was the river that made me want to fish again. When the weather was good I'd walk down to Memorial Square and find a high place to sit and look across FDR Drive at the tows and Coast Guard cutters coming up the channel. It was near the downtown heliport and, on especially hot days when there was nothing coming down The Drive, the only sounds were the APU's whining and the rotors turning up and changing pitch to fly. I'd look above the buildings and bridges where there was nothing but sky and it was like the first launch of Medivacs off the flight deck, climbing out across the ocean to the highlands beyond Chu Lai.

One lunchtime an old Harker's Island came up the channel, probably sightseeing. I hadn't seen one in years. It was a clear, windy day in late March and she was painted white and heavy-hulled the way all Carolina boats tended to be. I looked between the outriggers at the two men on the bridge and remembered that it was billfish season down in the islands. I also remembered a client of mine who was shopping for his first boat. I called him that afternoon and described Little Cay and said that if we talked a little business between marlin we could probably write off most of the trip. He was game and told me to count his son in, too, if I could make the arrangements.

I didn't know the contest was running or that *The Katherine* was there and I would see Sonny again. I didn't know Inez would be there either or that Ulis nearly always told the truth, I didn't know anything then.

* * * * *

I was on with a California client when my other line lit. Liz picked it up.

She turned around to face me. "Dave from Midwestern."

I held up a finger and finished the call. I picked up Dave.

"Get any rain yet?"

"Nothing like we need," he said. "Are you going to tell me all about Eastcom again?"

"Only its good points."

"Where is it?"

"Forty-four and three-eights, a half."

"We'll take a position. I wanted it at a quarter though."

I said, "Buyers showed up this morning. There's size ahead of us now. But, if you want to let an eighth stand in your way... "

He thought a moment.

"Go ahead and hit the bid."

"How much Dave?"

"Why don't you buy me twenty-five thousand shares."

"Will you take any part?"

"No less than ten."

"Thanks, sir. See you back." I punched the other line and called the block desk. A women answered.

"I have an order for Emil."

"Stay there," she said quickly.

A second later I heard his voice. "I'm on."

"It's Jim. I need to buy twenty-five thousand Eastcom at forty-four and three-eighths."

A line lit. Liz had it.

"Ciro," she said.

I held up a finger, while Emil wrote the ticket and read it back to me. Then he said, "There's fifty-thousand ahead of you."

"Fill me no less than ten thousand shares, Emil."

He grunted and I picked up Ciro.

"Do we have bait?" Ciro asked.

"Two hundred dollars worth. Big and small ballyhoo, big and small mullet. Big mackerel and really big squid. Wait'll you see this squid. It's half as long as the boat."

"Speaking of which, tell me about this guy we hired."

"He's a Bahamian. We'll save a few bucks. All the American boats are booked anyway. He'll run over from Nassau and meet us on the Cay tomorrow night. He's got a thirty-eight foot Cubavitch."

"Is that good?"

"A Cubavitch is a good boat, Ciro. Also it's a little smaller than most charter boats so we'll save on fuel."

"Could you get the extra room?"

"They're working on it. If not, you and your son take the one and I'll sleep on the boat. They're jammed up with the tournament."

"What tournament?"

"The marlin tournament. It runs both days we'll be there."

"Can we enter it?"

"I guess we can. There'll be an entry fee."

My line lit. Liz turned around.

"Emil says it's your bid."

I motioned thanks and spoke to Ciro.

"I guess we're set."

"Um-hum."

"While I have you, Eastcom got very cheap the last few days. Why don't we add to it?"

"Do I have any cash?"

"Enough for about seven hundred."

"Do it then."

"Okay, boss. I'll meet you on the plane. Don't forget your passports."

"Ciao," he said.

I wrote out a market order for seven hundred shares and looked at it. Then Emil called.

"You bought nineteen-thousand three hundred Eastcom at forty-four and three-eighths."

"Nice fill, Emil, sit on the rest." I hit the keys on my quote machine and saw the bid was up a half point to 44 7/8.

"Headed north," I said into the phone. "Aren't we smart?"

"Yeah," he laughed sarcastically. "That's why we're here."

* * * * *

Pete Reed taught me to fish the summers I worked for him after my father died. He helped my mother sell our boat and hired me as his mate even though I was only fourteen.

"You may know boats," he told me, "but don't think you'll get top dollar until you learn to fish."

I was paid seven dollars a day plus tips when we had charters. Pete was booked nearly every day, the only for-hire boat permitted at our exclusive yacht basin. He was one of the few men in those days who made money in the charter business and he brought the boat south to fish the winters in Florida.

In four years I learned the trade. We trolled for school tuna and bluefish and ran offshore in the late summer for billfish. Those were the best trips, sixty or seventy miles out where the Gulf Stream ran over the little canyons of the Northern shelf. We would leave at midnight, churning out at half-speed away from the glare of the beach. While the clients slept below, Pete and I split wheel watches on the bridge under trails of almost continuous shooting stars. Sometimes there were the festive lights of a liner for company or the smaller, serious ones of a tanker, but most of the time there was nothing in the night except hundreds of miles of dark ocean around us.

By first light, we'd be through the steamer lanes and could run the last twenty miles. We knew when we hit the Gulf Stream as clearly as if it were marked with a buoy. It was deeper blue than the other ocean and it moved differently, not always obedient to the wind.

There was no telling what we would catch out there. Bluefin and yellowfin tuna, dolphin, white and blue marlin, we raised a big swordfish one dusk and couldn't make him strike, but did hook a nice mako a little later who gave us a show. Makos are the only sharks you can catch trolling and, to my knowledge, the only ones that jump.

At night we'd drift and drop squid fifty or sixty fathoms for tilefish. We had to use a lot of lead to get the bait that deep, mostly old sash weights from windows and it was a job cranking all that line in with or without a fish. I was always sad to see the strange-looking bottom fish come up choking on their enlarged insides, the pressure of 300 feet of water suddenly off them. But they died quickly in the cockpit and were delicious. Years later I saw them sold in New York fish stores as ocean perch.

We lost a set line out there one morning and wasted the rest of the day trying to find it, had a swearing match with a Russian tuna boat that decided to set its net around a school of bluefin we happened to be in and, in the middle of a windless night, started the engines and ran from an empty freighter bearing down on our little lights. She was light and probably so high out of the water that we must have been under her radar when she closed on us. She went by like a building and I nearly flew off the bridge when we rolled in her wake.

We were careful about weather but were fooled badly, once, by a Northwester that blew up during the night. It would have been bad enough near the beach but where we were it raised mountains around us. The rain stopped at daylight but the blow got worse. It was too rough to troll or do anything else except try to keep the bow into it. Seas broke around us, crashing like snow-covered hills, but the sky was brilliant. I learned to look at the sky whenever I thought about how small we were and how far from land. The bilge pump never stopped running that day and we used almost all our reserve fuel keeping the boat straight. It was the worst beating I ever took in a boat, and when it was over, it had blown us thirty more miles offshore.

When it came time for college, I applied to a school in Florida so I could fish the weekends with Pete when he brought the boat south. It worked out pretty well. I wasn't much of a student, but managed passing grades, remarkable, considering the number of classes I cut when the sailfishing was hot.

In the spring semester, Pete brought the boat north early to haul out and get ready for the summer. While the work was being done, he'd pick up a few days running Bud Hillery's Fortesque, one of the last charter boats in the river that hadn't gone to diesel. It wasn't much of a boat, most of it was dry-rotting faster than the wood could be replaced.

Buddy fitted a new bulkhead himself the week before Pete took her out. He must have driven a nail through it and into the top third of a fuel tank. Nobody smelled gas because the tanks weren't full. Pete fueled the morning he was taking a charter out. He opened the hatches and started both engines and closed them up, idling in the slip. Warmed up, the mate cast her off and they headed out the line of boats at the dock and into the channel.

It took about that long to get the right mixture of air in the bilge, the tank leaked about a teacup. A stray spark, probably from the generator, set it off. The bilge and the rest of the gas blew in the middle of the channel. They fished out the mate, the only one, who'd been standing on the gunwale, putting the outriggers down. When the boat started drifting toward the dock they threw a grapple into the fire and towed her back out to the channel. The line burned through and popped and she started to drift again so they used a good anchor with twenty feet of chain. They towed her out a second time and held her there until she burned to the waterline.

If I loved anyone they never lasted long. I finished the semester and stayed in Miami, bumming around the shipyards for work and getting drunk in the rundown places along the river. In the fall I joined the Navy. I just wanted to look at water I didn't already know, a different ocean.

CHAPTER II

Ciro ran down the aisle like a little bulldog, chasing his son. The plane had boarded and I was about to leave a message that I would wait for them in Nassau. They handed the attendant their boarding passes. Ciro was flushed and panting.

"After two years of college my scholarly son can't set an alarm clock."

We hurried on the plane and I stuck out my hand. "Glad to meet you, Michael."

"Nice to meet you. Sorry we're late." He was a pleasant looking kid with light brown hair and a mustache. He probably took after his mother and wouldn't lose his hair like Ciro.

I told Ciro he looked like he'd lost weight.

"Sixteen pounds. I cut back on the silver bullets."

"The what?"

"Martinis."

It was a nice day to fly. The seats on either side of mine were empty and I went through a few magazines, had breakfast and the lousy airline coffee. I started back to chat a few times but Ciro and his son never regained consciousness. Sunlight poured through the cabin windows and I dozed on and off, the last time for twenty minutes or so. I felt the plane change and we started to drop. Grand Bahama Island sprawled below, West End jutting out like a manta's tail. We crossed the channel to the wave-lined sand flats of The Great Bank. Andros Island rose from the bank, broke in half and ran forty more miles, the jagged pieces as perfect as they looked on the chart. We turned east and the bottom disappeared again, the sea ran indigo bright and a windy island of small pines appeared. Nassau.

Even before we touched down everything was different, the clear, lazy sunlight, the heavy sea-filled air. Like the shine of The South China Sea, but with none of the dread, it was all so good again. I looked behind at Ciro and Michael as we taxied to the apron. The landing had jarred them awake. With our carry-ons we debarked to the sunlight and headed for customs.

I saw the sweat form on Michael as he turned to speak to me.

"You're going to have to coach me on this deep-sea business. The biggest fish I've ever caught is a largemouth bass."

"It can be monotonous at times," I said, "but there's no better action when a fish is on. We'll troll rigged bait very slowly and watch for a fish to strike." I looked completely around us. "Let's hope the weather holds. The less wind the better."

Ciro said, "I came through Nassau years ago on my way back from Cuba."

"Before my time?" asked Michael.

"Way before, I wasn't even married yet. Your Uncle Jack hit the trifecta and we both went. Havana was something then, we had a fucking ball."

When our passports were stamped we headed for the baggage claim. Michael and I signaled whenever we saw an attractive girl. All were his age with their families or in little groups headed for one resort or another. There weren't very many. It wasn't really tourist season. Our bags came up along with the two cardboard boxes I'd packed the bait in.

Michael asked me if the bait was still frozen.

"Yup. I lined those boxes with styrofoam sheets. It'll stay hard a few more days packed like that."

"Wouldn't it have been easier to buy the bait down here?"

"You can't get good bait in the islands. What little you find fresh costs twice as much, I had ours air-freighted up from Miami. I repacked it and added some dry ice. A lot of work, but it's worth its weight in gold down here."

"Maybe we should get into the bait business," said Ciro.

I shouldered a box. "I think I'll stay on Wall Street a little longer."

Michael and I hauled everything to customs. We were the last ones from the flight and must have looked suspicious to the two Bahamian officers at the counter. The younger of the two eyed the bait boxes.

"What's in there?"

"Mackerel, squid, mullet, and ballyhoo," I said, "frozen bait."

He looked at Ciro and back to me.

"Open it."

"All right, but we'll have to seal it back up. Do you have any tape?"

"No. No tape."

"Then we'll have to find some." I grabbed Michael and we cased each little shop in the airport. A profiteering liquor store clerk sold us a skimpy roll for five dollars U.S.

Ciro stood off to one side with the luggage.

"The rum may be cheap down here," I said, "but the tape's a dollar a foot."

"They're in cahoots with customs."

"It's your bushy eyebrows, Ciro. He thinks you're a Mafia Don and that Michael and me are your bag men."

"He can't think there's dope in the boxes," Michael said. "They're ice cold."

"Stiffs," I said. "He thinks we're bringing down the remains of some stool pigeon for a sea burial."

Ciro said, "I'll rattle off a few Sicilian oaths to add to the drama."

We carried the boxes up for the second time and Ciro used his little knife to slit one. A dry ice cloud swirled up and we all looked at the little fish. The officer nodded and Michael taped it shut.

"Open the other one."

"Christ," I said under my breath. "I hope we have enough tape."

The big squid were in the second box. It took the officers a minute to be sure they weren't plastic bags full of something purple and illegal.

"Okay, okay," the senior one finally said. "Enjoy your trip."

"Gee, thanks," said Ciro.

We found a sky cap and loaded him up.

"I'd like to know how you got that knife through the metal detector at La Guardia," I said.

"Depends on how they have the gain set. Sometimes it sets the alarm off sometimes it doesn't."

"Comforting."

Back out in the sunlight, we flagged a hulking, black 60's Cadillac. We packed the trunk and drove around looking for the

Island Air Service terminal that I had been told was close to the main building. We passed a dingy, pink, quonset hut twice before Michael noticed the row of Cessnas and Pipers behind it.

The driver charged us nine dollars U.S.

"We only went a half mile," Ciro told him.

"Back and forth so many times to find it," the driver said.

"How can you not know where it is if you drive around here all the time?" I asked him.

"Why should I know? It's you want to go here, Mon, not me."

We carried the bait boxes into the shade and went up the steps through the screen door. There was a tiny waiting room inside. On one wall, aviation sectional charts had been expertly pieced together to represent the entire Caribbean, Nassau was at the center, connected to each Bahama Island by a long thin pen line and compass heading. I followed one to the Northwest and found Little Cay.

"Here it is, Sportsmen," I said.

"I hope you chartered us a twin," said Ciro, looking at all the water on the chart. He held an instrument rating and still owned a plane.

We heard our names being called then, rhythmically, island-slow and we turned a corner looking for the voice. Behind a halfdoor with a flattened top, a thin Bahamian sat looking at a ticket book.

"The plane will take you now to Little Cay," he said.

Ciro and I wrote our checks and we lugged everything out to the apron where a young Bahamian pilot in sharp khakis finished pre-flighting a Piper Aztec. It was painted yellow with brown fuel tanks. The pilot stowed the bait and Ciro's big suitcase in a rear compartment. I started to shove my bag in but the pilot took it from me and walked around the wing. He used a key to open a forward compartment.

"Forget your weight and balances already?" Ciro asked me.

"Guess I'll always be a helicopter man," I said.

"You're a helicopter pilot?" asked Michael.

"Not a pilot. I crewed in one a few years back."

"Where?"

I thought for a moment which way west was and pointed a thumb behind me.

"Back there. Asia."

"He started to asked me something else but I nudged his shoulder and we climbed the wing strut. Everything in the cockpit was faded from the sun.

"You better sit up front," I called out to Ciro.

He nodded, climbing up, all trace of levity, wheeler-dealer gone. All three of us could take the controls if need be but he was the only one with a multi-engine rating. I watched him strap in and follow the charter pilot through the checklist.

The pilot yelled out the hatch, shut it and fired the engines. The needles rocked on the instrument panel and we smoothed out and started to taxi.

We crossed the runway threshold and turned into the wind and the Bahamian moved the throttles, first a touch to start the roll, then all the way up and we were racing low and loud and suddenly smooth, ascending over trees and beach and deepening shallows. We leveled off at sixty-five hundred feet, incredibly small in the sky and sea below us. Beyond the nose I couldn't find the horizon in the light blue.

"Can't tell the sky from the ocean out there," I shouted to Ciro above the engines.

He pointed to the horizon indicator on the panel.

"They've lost a few planes over the water on days like this."

And at night, too, I thought, *with the carrier lights blacked out. Exhausted crews heading back from eighteen hours of flying wounded. Pilot dozing off or simply flying it into the drink. Then, after, looking for the strobes. There was never much on top, only what hung crushed in the vests, impact lights merrily blinking, most of them younger than the Bahamian pilot flying this plane. Search and Rescue NATOPS called it. Medivacing the medivacs we used to say. When two birds collided one night over a splash we called it Triple M. The best thing about a helicopter going down in water was that there was no fire.*

I saw clouds then, to the left, holding close and low to the water. They had to be over a land mass.

"Island," I said and pointed.

"Andros," the pilot shouted over the hum.

Empty beaches rose up from sand banks and slid behind. There were long reefs in deeper water on the windward side and a few small skiffs working them. At once the bottom disappeared and became the color of cobalt.

Something splashed below us, we all got a glimpse before it slipped under the wing. It was a sport-fishing boat. I saw the tuna tower buck with a sea and white water flew.

"Boy's got outriggers and a tower. That's a fishing machine, gentlemen," I said, wacking Ciro with one hand and his son with the other.

"Is he fishing now?" Michael asked.

I shook my head. "Running," I shouted.

We saw more wakes and followed them like trails to the boats. The kid trimmed the nose and we started down. They were boats I hadn't seen the like of for years. All were painted white and had the set back and rigged look of serious sport-fishing. I wouldn't let myself think of my father then or of Pete or of other oceans or anything else. I listened to us throttle back and kept my head down to the water behind the plane. The last boat we flew over had no wake behind him and his outriggers were down.

"He's trolling in," I said.

We were low, less than 400 feet and I almost read the name on the transom. A man in a bright green shirt stood in the cockpit. The pilot dipped a wing and the man waved. I looked up, grinning, and saw Little Cay for the first time.

We flew up through the little inlet and over the docks and bounced once in a thermal. I felt the drag of the landing gear and the runway appeared, unbelievably narrow, in a brushy clearing. The kid cut everything and floated us down over the numbers. He held us off until the plane quit flying and, even in the heat, there was no jolt, we just heard the wheels hum and all three of us nodded.

"Bravo, bravo," Ciro bellowed, his seriousness gone now on the ground and the pilot smiled, kicking the tail around, heading us off the tarmac and onto the grass.

"They know you landed," the kid said. "Someone will come." He helped us unload, fired back up and taxied away with a wave. We followed him through his runup, then he was sailing by us again and off the runway like a cannonshot, flaunting his empty weight. He stayed low, swung back around, building speed, and buzzed us with a roaring climb that arched out over the docks.

"He's light on the controls, that kid," Ciro said.

I nodded. "He can fly that airplane."

We stood bareheaded in the sun.

"Which way's town?" Michael asked.

"On the other side of the Cay, but it isn't much. The marina's the only thing at this end. If you didn't come to fish you'd be pretty bored around here."

"How about scuba diving?"

"The inshore reefs probably aren't much better than Nassau so nobody comes out here to dive."

"What makes the fishing so great?"

"The Cay's on the edge of a deep water channel called The Tongue. The currents funnel the nutrients from the surrounding ocean down through here."

"You sound like a goddamn marine biologist," Ciro said.

"So, the nutrients attract marlin and stuff," said Michael.

"The nutrients attract bait which attracts gamefish, marlin and stuff."

"Which attracts us," added Ciro.

"How many times have you been down here?" Michael asked.

"This is my first."

"How do you know so much about it, then?"

"My father fished here when he was alive. Said it was the best place ever if the conditions were right."

Ciro looked at me.

"How would the conditions happen to be, right now?"

"Seem to be okay. Looks like we'll know pretty soon," I pointed.

A pickup truck that may have been maroon before the sun turned it brown, creaked along the edge of the clearing. The driver, an elderly island man, wore a faded blue golf cap and bounced up, wrestling the wheel. He stopped, shut off the motor and grinned. He was black as coal.

"Three men here to raise hell," he said, looking us over.

"Any to be raised?" Ciro asked him.

"Some," he nodded, getting out. "Some to raise with the boats coming in and the tournament on."

We loaded everything in the back of the truck and I climbed up with Michael and sat with the stuff. Ciro rode up front with the driver. We bounced across the clearing to a two-tracked sand road that led us into trees, mostly pines. The sand road was covered with their needles. We rode in the shade of the trees until they thinned out on Ciro's side and we saw the ocean.

From the opened window he said to me, "This is a nice spot, Jim."

The trees went dark around us again and were interspersed with palmettos covered with thick brown moss. Little birds flew from the moss and glided deeper in, away from the road.

The nose of the truck dipped, Michael and I followed it down, and we slid across a muddy bottom of black muck and back up. A creek. There were banana trees growing on either side of us. They were shorter than the pines and greener in the sun.

A quarter mile beyond the creek, probably less, we were riding so slow, we broke out of the trees onto a real dirt road. We followed it around a bend in the scrub and I saw the line of outriggers from the docked boats, the back of the commissary and the restaurant.

"Gentlemen, The Little Cay Club," I announced.

"All *right*," said Michael.

We rode around to the little office and registered, but the additional room wasn't available.

I shrugged. "I'll just dump my stuff in your room for now and sleep on the boat."

Ciro was hot on getting into the tournament so we entered as one crew and were given caps, copies of the rules, and a green flag to fly.

We went back out to the truck and stood waiting for the driver to come back and haul us to the room. I could see the superstructures of the closest boats docked in a line down from the office. Ciro flipped through the little rule book.

Half a dozen boats had come through the inlet. They held steady in the light current, waiting for a turn at the gas dock at the far end of the marina.

"How many boats do you think will fish this tournament?" Ciro asked me.

"Twenty. Twenty-five." I looked back to the boats tied closest to us. I started to say something but stopped. I was looking at the bridge and wheelhouse of an exceptionally well-kept Rybovitch. A small lifering was mounted on the side of the bridge with the name of the boat painted on in gold letters. I couldn't read it but recognized the little crossed pennant insignia at the beginning and end of the name. Something like a wave rolled up and broke in my chest.

"Jesus."

"What?" asked Ciro.

It took me a moment to answer.

"Nothing. I used to know that boat, I think."

Our driver came back smiling and I climbed up onto the truck and waved for Michael to walk back. When he was up in the truck and sitting on the sides, I pointed to the boat.

"Did you see the name on that Rybovitch?"

"That what?"

"That boat, it's a Rybovitch," I pointed. "Did you see the name on the transom, the back end?"

"I can't remember, Jim."

"Look at the flying bridge. See the lifering? Can you read the name on that?"

Michael squinted. "It's one word or one word and a letter."

"Katherine H.?"

The truck started up and we headed off the other way toward the rooms.

"I can't say," Michael answered, still squinting.

We bumped in a pothole and I held to the side. I didn't have to ask Michael. I knew those lines. It had to be *The Katherine*.

CHAPTER III

Inez Hutchinson roomed with my older sister their first year of college. Her family kept their boat at the same marina ours had. I was always around there in the summers, fishing or helping my father with something and, later, when our boat was sold, working for Pete. The Hutchinsons were wealthy. Inez's father, Richard, was the grandson of a major steelmaker. His boat, *The Katherine H.*, was a well-made classic sportfisherman quite unlike the more extravagant versions owned by his contemporaries. He and his wife, Katherine, made quite a few tournaments in those days. They didn't need a top-heavy yacht, there were enough hotels in Ocean City or Montauk. Living on board with the crew was a touch intimate, anyway. An average-looking man, Hutchinson traveled to Caracas in his late twenties on one business or another, and met his first wife, Christine, the daughter of an American Ambassador and his Venezuelan bride. They were married and established permanent residence in Bucks County, Pennsylvania, near his family's interests.

Christine died of something in her thirties, I never found out what. A full five years later, before we'd known him, Hutchinson married Katherine Rowe of Newport, Rhode Island. "Clubby Kate," I heard someone once say. Actually, the few times Kate Hutchinson spoke to me around the dock she was very nice. Inez never referred to her any other way than as her stepmother. My folks knew them casually, well enough to chat a bit at the marina or at parties, but I don't think anyone concerned with bills and things ever got to know the Hutchinsons very well.

Before she went to school with my sister, I'd seen Inez about a dozen times over the years. She was a quiet girl with those she didn't know and favored her South American mother. When she was younger and slightly frail, I thought she looked at me from out of the corner of her eye. As awkward as I was I invented reasons to walk by her boat and if she looked at me then, with her mother's sweet, dark eyes, I was sure she was hiding something. I knew what it was after my father died. It was simply loneliness and I loved her for it.

Inez began to appear around our house in the time before she and my sister started school. She came to the funeral but I don't recall that her parents did. She was nice enough to us, though, looking back, I doubt she and my sister were very close. They smoked cigarettes at the dining room table, drinking tea and talking about design. They were fashion majors. If I played my cards right and my sister was feeling charitable, I was free to sit with them as long as I didn't say much. Around my sister I thought Inez wanted to treat me like a mascot but couldn't quite. I was a big kid at fifteen and sixteen and, once in private, my mother kind of matter-of-factly mentioned it was a shame Inez was three years older than me. That was one summer afternoon. Inez had come by early and sat in the back yard with me talking about a lot of things until my sister got home and they went someplace. My mother had looked out at us now and then through the kitchen screens and said it to me later that evening as she fixed my dinner.

Toward the end of the following summer I was sixteen and the Hutchinson's captain, Sonny Sherwood, asked me if I wanted to mate for him the first week of September. Pete brought his boat south at the end of August and I usually took that week off as it was the last before school started. Sonny was running the boat up to Cape Cod where Mr. and Mrs. Hutchinson would fish The Invitational Tuna Tournament. I'd never been all the way up to The Cape and decided to go at Pete's suggestion that, if nothing else, it would be good navigating experience.

Sonny knew boats and managed to keep *The Katherine H.* spotless, but was nonetheless one of the laziest men any of us knew and one of the biggest drinkers. He varnished and painted a little when the mood struck him but acted more as a subcontractor when anything strenuous needed doing. He'd hire kids like me to scrub and polish and, since he had no ambition to attempt the simplest repairs, a mechanic was on board often enough to seem permanently stationed. He was also unbelievably negligent, at times, and once almost sank the boat when he left the lines too tight during a moon tide. The stern drifted under the dock, wedged in and couldn't rise as the water got high. Her scuppers went under and we found her cockpit half full in the morning. Pete was as amused with Sonny as anyone, saying, if *The Katherine* sank Sonny'd be wise to go down with her because nobody else would hire him.

We left for Cape Cod the morning of September 1st, just Sonny and I on board. The Hutchinsons would meet us on The Cape. We started late, I remember, Sonny had made his rounds the night before. Most of the charter fleet was well out of sight by the time we cleared the jetty.

Red-eyed, Sonny gave me the wheel just beyond the range buoys and went below for a nap. *The Katherine* was a fast boat and I headed her northeast full of pride and responsibility, eyes alternating between the compass, the horizon, and just beyond the bow for floating timber.

It was one of those times when everything was on top. Tuna broke around me all morning, I could have walked on them, and I saw a whale come up and blow. The spout vaporized and hung like a fish-smelling cloud and I swung the boat for a closer look but turned back on coarse when two smaller shapes breached near it. Pete had always warned me not to push one with her calves.

It was the kind of day you remember for years, I still think about it. I was young then and clean in the head, alone on the bridge of a wonderful boat and running it across open water to a place I'd never seen. The world was right that morning and, hours later, after Moriches was in sight, low and white in the sun, I edged in closer to the beach and ran her fifty more miles. It was noon when Sonny came up, yawning. He took the wheel but I stayed on the bridge, watching the swells of grass-covered dunes and birds dive from the rocks of the jettys we passed. It was cooler the farther up we ran and I saw Montauk, the big red and white striped lighthouse high on the point a full half minute before him.

It took another day to get the boat to Cape Cod, mostly running inside, through channels, including the longest stretch of canal I'd ever seen, until we broke through to the bay.

We tied up in Provincetown and Mr. and Mrs. Hutchinson met us on the dock. Inez had come up with them and was staying with friends in Hyannis. Sonny and I bought bait and chum and put new dacron line on the big twelve O reels.

It was flat calm the first day and very hot. Fishing for big tuna was rather dull, you anchored or drifted if it was too deep and ladled out ground fish chum until you had a pretty good slick behind the boat. The smell of the chum in the water was supposed to attract the tuna. You drifted two lines baited with whole mackerel through the slick and waited. Sonny sat up on the bridge in the shade of the canvas top with Hutchinson, and Mrs. H. read in the cool of the wheelhouse, coming out through the open door every half hour to smile at me and wet herself from a bucket of seawater.

We thought we had some action that afternoon but it was only a blue shark playing with one of the mackerel. I could see him thirty feet down in the blue, swishing that tail around as he looked over the bait. I told Sonny and he and Hutchinson agreed it would be good practice for Mrs. H. to catch the shark.

Mrs. H. marked her place in the novel she was reading and sauntered out to the cockpit. She was just getting in the fighting chair when the shark hit the mackerel hard. It wasn't a tournament fish so I set the hook myself and walked the heavy rod to Mrs. H. in the chair. When I was sure she had the rod butt in the gimbal, I worked the harness up under her and buckled it to the reel. It would keep her and the tackle from being pulled over.

Sonny started both engines and he and Mr. Hutchinson started yelling to get the anchor line loose. I scrambled up on the bow and uncleated the line and threw it over with the orange buoy made fast. It was quicker than trying to pull the anchor up with a fish on.

The shark was taking line. He didn't run like a game fish but pulled as sharks did, moronically and like a dead weight in the same direction. Mrs. H. knew enough not to struggle with him. When he stopped stripping line Sonny used the boat to work on him. He idled both engines in reverse while Mrs. H. got back line. It was hard work in the heat and I admired the way she kept at it. As they sometimes do, the shark turned and swam in the same direction he was being pulled, probably out of curiosity. He came up, following us behind the stern with that mean-looking double slice of tail and dorsal fin. Sonny took the boat out of gear and I reached for the leader when it came and pulled him in side-handed. I was surprised how easily he came. I was so sure the shark was finished that I took a double wrap of the wire around my palm to haul him in faster. Just then he lost his curiosity in the boat and made a U-turn with absolutely no effort. The leader nearly shredded the glove from my hand, I remember looking to see if I'd lost a finger. Then I looked up at Sonny who was shaking his head. Pete would have given me an ass chewing. Taking a wrap like that could cripple you if a fish was still green.

Sonny backed down and Mrs. H. reeled and we finally got the shark behind the boat. Sonny came down and tagged him and I cut the leader as close to his mouth as I dared, the hook would rust out in a few weeks. We got everything together, retrieved the anchorline, and got back on our chumslick. I put out two fresh mackerel and in five minutes the same shark was nosing around them, circling to strike. I could see the orange tag and the leader wire trailing off his gills. I asked Sonny if we wanted to catch him again and he told me to pull up the anchor, that there wouldn't be any tuna around now that our friend had laid claim to the slick.

The second day Inez came out with us. The sun was just as strong but there was a little more wind and she alternated between sunbathing on the bow, reading in the wheelhouse, and sitting on the bridge with her father and Sonny. She smiled at me now and then and made me a couple of sandwiches in the after-noon but we didn't really talk. We just couldn't raise a tunafish. Toward dusk we called it quits. I brought in the lines and we started in. Suddenly the flat water off the starboard grew humps and fins. We'd found a school, bunched up and moving together. I'd never seen anything like it; they looked as huge as whales. Anyone who fishes for smaller school tuna will tell you when you see them break water they're almost impossible to catch and it was no different with these gi-ants. There wasn't anything swimming in that school under 400 pounds. I put out a mackerel and a squid and we trolled along-side them or directly across but they spooked every time and changed direction. I was going crazy. After not seeing anything for two days I was thirty or forty yards from these enormous fish, so close I could see their blue and silver backs in the fading light, but I couldn't make them strike. We must have chased them for thirty minutes, they didn't go down but simply turned away from us whenever we came. Desperate, I reeled in the mackerel, peeled a hundred feet of line off into the cockpit and hurled the bait by hand over the school. The line trailed out in a splendid arc and Mr. Hutchinson was pretty impressed. I tried it a dozen more times until Sonny told me that nothing would work, there was no way to catch the fish. We watched them head up like cattle and roll off to the south with the sun going down. Inez and I looked at each other. I was sure she knew how I felt. When the fish were out of sight we hooked up and ran the rest of the way in, slowly.

Mr. Hutchinson made a phone call that evening and sud-denly had to do something in New York the following day, which was Monday. He decided to fly down in the morning. Sonny and I would bring the boat back with Inez and Mrs. H. on board.

The breeze that started the day before picked up in the night. Cape Cod Bay was still calm in the morning but, heading out the inlet, I saw the highest flags on the beach out straight and I knew it had to be rough offshore. Hours later, halfway through the canal, the sky went completely gray. I went below to shut all the hatches and checked the barometer which had fallen. We found a weather station on the ship to shore and, by noon, small craft conditions had deteriorated to gale with a hurricane watch in effect.

"I'd like to get as far as Montauk if we have to wait it out," Sonny said.

Out of the canal, in open water, the seas had become monstrous. There was no land to break that cauldron of wind from the southeast. There was no better sea boat for her size than *The Katherine* with her three foot keel, but she trembled with every sea, kicking the stern so high the shafts and props flew free, cavitated with a roar louder than the wind, and slammed back down to the next sea. Sonny pointed the bow for Montauk and cut the engines to a third to keep us together. Even running slow we were completely soaked with spray.

I went down to check on Inez and Mrs. H. and found them sorting out the avalanche of rods and charts that had come loose from the brackets. I dug out life jackets and foul weather gear for me and Sonny, switched the bilge pump to automatic, and started back up for the bridge. Inez wanted to come back up with me. She looked frightened, but excited. I agreed to take her up, mostly because I knew how dangerous it could be for someone below if they fell or hit their head. We were really heaving. I looked at Mrs. H.

"She could get banged up pretty badly down here," I shouted, as a quartering sea took us up like a rocket, hung us a moment, and dropped us with a smack.

"All right, Jim, but please, please don't let her go overboard."

"I won't, ma'am."

I dug out a life jacket and fitted it to her as best I could and buttoned a yellow foul weather top over it.

"Don't bother with the bottoms, you're going to get soaked anyway."

From the flarebox I took a small plastic device a little bigger than a cigarette pack.

"Know what this is?" I asked Inez.

"Flashlight?"

"Close. It's a strobe. It's water activated. Put it in your back pocket. If you wind up in the water dig it out and clip it to your life vest."

Inez looked at it and put it where I told her.

I rooted around for the canned airhorn and handed it to Mrs. Hutchinson.

"If you need us, Mrs. H., just hit this toggle like so."

The high-pitched whine was deafening in the wheelhouse.

I took Inez's arm. "Come on."

I led her through the wheelhouse hatch, latched it shut behind us, and went around to the ladder. One thing I always liked about that boat was that the ladder to the bridge was mounted alongside the wheelhouse, leaving the cockpit unobstructed. It was a perfect setup for fighting a fish but hairy going in fledgling hurricane. Sheets of water drenched us as we made our way.

"Oh my God," I heard Inez say.

I went up on the gunwale first, gripped the ladder and held myself out away from it.

"C'mon," I yelled to her.

She climbed up the ladder inside of me, stopping when a bad sea had us. I went up even with her and we staggered over the bridge deck. I wedged her in alongside Sonny and stood behind them, holding on with one hand. With the other, I untied Sonny's lifevest from my belt and helped him put it on. I could tell he was mad at me for bringing Inez on top.

Inez was looking at the ocean around her. I saw her say, "My God," again but couldn't hear her in the wind. The ocean was gray and churning with broken seas. From under the stuff blowing on top, huge, irregular ground seas welled up at us but the surface was so rough you couldn't see them. The sky was dark, it was probably raining, but so much spray was flying I couldn't tell.

I screamed to Inez. "Are you okay?"

She nodded that she was.

At least eight miles off, a single bolt of lightning split the gray sky down to the sea. Inez trembled once but I knew she wasn't afraid. If not for Sonny, I would have brought her close to me. Instead, I put my free hand on her shoulder and it looked as though I was steadying her.

The bow shot up with another sea. I didn't dodge the spray this time and saw Block Island as we came down.

"It's a freak wind, this southeast," Sonny shouted. He swung the bow back, keeping the island to port, heading us for the west side. Block Island was as far as we'd get.

Steering was horrid. Sonny and I split fifteen minute wheel watches. I went down once to tell Mrs. Hutchinson we were almost up to the island. She had gone forward and wedged herself in a lower bunk with cushions. Pale as she was, she smiled when she saw me. I told her Inez was fine on the bridge and went back up and took the wheel from Sonny. He had to use the head but was afraid to go down. He staggered behind us, to the end of the flopping bridge deck, turned a bit to get the wind right and un-zipped. Inez and I looked at him and laughed. His water disap-peared in the steady spray of sea water.

In another hour we were going around the island. I started seeing boats. The closest ones nearly cleared the water when a big sea took them up and we could see the blue or red-painted bottoms down to their keels as well as if they were drydocked.

It calmed down in the lee of the island. The terrific bucking stopped and it was a matter of rolling with the ground sea. The rain really started, smoothing the rollers and Sonny added a little power to round the island. I couldn't see the beach beneath the cliffs, the swells were too high. Yawing back from a roller, we saw the flash of the inlet beacon through the rain.

The high hills above the harbor were capped with rain clouds. Sonny kept us offshore, well out into the wind again before he turned for the inlet. There were no boats coming through, noth-ing was going out in this sea. In a storm, most boats that didn't make it through the inlet were lost in a following sea. There wasn't much steerage with a big wave behind you so you waited for the series of waves to break and tried in the lull.

The seas were coming in threes. When the third sent gey-sers fifty feet high and flooded the jetty rocks, Sonny pushed the throttles all the way to the corner. We charged the inlet with the sea chasing us.

With the wind behind I could hear the engines wail. The lull came and the reverse surge, the current running back out, held us like a vacuum. We crept up and were between the jetties when I turned around and saw a monster behind us. I whacked Sonny's shoulder and he glanced back and nodded. He'd expected it. Inez turned around.

"Oh God," she said.

It was a mother building up and coming at us like a canal bank.

In the moments before the wave, we hit slack current and gained a hundred yards or so, engines turning like demons. Then the mother sea drew us up. There was an awful hanging and I saw Sonny fight to keep the bow centered in the inlet. Suddenly, we were moving again, faster than I'd ever been in a boat. We slid down the sea like a toboggan, green water flying from the digging bow. Like a nose-first ride into a canyon, I looked behind and there was nothing but sky above the transom.

The rudders were useless. Sonny cut both throttles but the surge had us almost on top of the west jetty, I held Inez, ready to get her off some way if we lost the boat on the rocks.

Sonny opened the starboard throttle all the way and swung the wheel madly.

"You sonofabitch," he shouted.

I saw clumps of mussels growing on the black jetty rock and waited for the scraping sound.

Then we stopped as if frozen. The bow went up like a rocket and we actually slid back a touch. The wave had passed under us and played out on the rocks.

Slowly, the boat leveled and started to come around. Sonny gunned the other throttle. In a few moments we dug in again and were through the inlet to the harbor.

Inside, the currents were like nothing I had ever seen. We needed half throttle even to crawl in the channel. The harbor was full of sailboats with deeper keels that couldn't get in the shallower water to dock. They anchored on both sides of the channel, whipping against their anchor lines like wolves. Some had two anchors out, the lines strung taunt as piano wire. If any of them broke loose there was nothing they could do but try to stay in mid-harbor with the engines.

All the docks were completely full and on hurricane alert. We couldn't get a slip but a dock where they knew the boat gave us space along the inside bulkhead. Because of the emergency conditions, we were to let another boat raft alongside us if need be. Sonny hated to agree to it but there wasn't any choice.

He handled the boat remarkably well while I tied us up. It was good to see what he was capable of.

He shut the engines down and came off the bridge for the first time that day. He held a little conference with Mrs. H. and the dockmaster while Inez helped me finish up the lines. It was really raining now and we were both soaked. Mrs. Hutchinson called us into the wheelhouse to dry off and we had tea and sand-wiches. The wind howled through the outriggers and the rain hit the side windows like cannon.

I looked at Inez in the wheelhouse light, safe now, out of the wind. We had come through something, the two of us, and would go through something more before it was over.

Sonny and I spent the afternoon doubling up lines and rig-ging dock bumpers. The rain eased a bit, but the wind was get-ting worse, much worse. Some of the boats rafted together started smacking each other and the dock creaked and swayed. Mrs. Hutchinson went to the marina office, the only thing around that wasn't rocking, and called every hotel on the island for a room. Sonny hired a taxi to take him to a junkyard and came back with old tires bulging from the trunk and back seat. We rolled them down the dock and tied them together to use as extra bumpers.

Before dusk, the dockmaster came down in the rain to tell us he had to raft a boat to us. Sonny and I got busy with the tires and a 45-foot Pacemaker drifted up too fast and turned quickly, churning against the current. The guy on the bridge, obviously terrified, was alone with his wife. They had come from our tournament at The Cape. There was no way the two of them could tie her up in that wind so he made a pass close to the leeward side of the dock and Sonny and I hopped aboard. We dug out his docklines from below and rigged him to come alongside. Sonny talked him through the maneuver about as gently as was possible for him and we managed to get a bowline on *The Katherine* and warp the Pacemaker alongside. We rigged spring and stern lines and the rest of the tires. The man, a doctor from Long Island, didn't have any bumpers but plenty of lifejackets so we bundled them and used them with the tires to keep the two boats apart. Mrs. H. came down the row of pilings holding onto the dockmaster to keep from being blown into the water.

"Inez," she announced in the rain, "it appears we are stuck on the goddamn boat tonight with the rest of the crew."

She and Inez went aboard the Pacemaker and struck up an immediate comraderie with the doctor's wife who had been completely drenched despite her foul weather gear.

When we had the boats as secure and double-lined as we could, we all hopped aboard the Pacemaker which was more yacht-like and had a huge wheelhouse and galley. Mrs. H. and the doctor's wife pooled provisions and whipped up a very nice dinner of hamburgers, fresh tuna salad, and canned corn. Afterwards, Sonny discussed the weather with the doctor. I was thinking it would probably be one of the few nights in his adult life he'd spend completely sober when the doctor hauled out a bottle of scotch. They had about three each.

At about nine, we went back to *The Katherine* in the rain. The tide had dropped us below the bulkhead but the wind was gusting forty knots. Out in the channel, anchored boats bucked like horses, the harbor was rough as an ocean and the mastlights whipped in the wind. Sonny and I checked the lines and bumpers, she was riding pretty well against the doctor's boat. Mrs. H. went down to the master stateroom all the way in the bow and Sonny took the little bunkroom we split next to the head. Inez and I found an FM frequency on the ship to shore and stayed up playing scrabble and listening to rock and roll. She didn't say much except to sing parts of songs she liked. At eleven she went below to the master stateroom. I thought I'd better stay up above so I undressed and stretched out with a blanket and cushion on the wheelhouse carpet. I checked the barometer. It was still dropping and I cut out the light.

I was dead tired from the run down and fell asleep quickly. Sometime after two, there was a tremendous slam and I sat up, not knowing where I was. I heard another noise, wood on wood followed by another slamming almost as hard. I thought first the tide must have raised us, slacking the dock lines so we knocked the bulkhead. I found the light and had my trousers up when I saw Inez in the ladderway, fully dressed.

"What's hitting us?" she asked me.

"I'm going out to look now." I put on my foul weather gear and watched her unhook hers from the top of the wheelhouse door.

"What do you think you're doing?"

"I want to come."

I didn't protest. I helped her snap up and slid the wheelhouse door open. The wind was incredible, we were out of most of it, down low and in the lee of the bulkhead, the hurricane was close, as close as it would come. Something slammed the boat again, we couldn't hear it in the howl, but felt it through the deck. Holding Inez to me, we climbed up on the bridge. In the beam of the docklight in the rain we saw the mast of a sailboat rocking madly between our hull and the hull of the Pacemaker. I guided us back down to the cockpit. Sonny was at the wheelhouse door in a T-shirt.

"What the hell's that racket?" he shouted.

"A sailboat got loose," I screamed back, "she's between us to the spring cleats."

When his raingear was on, the three of us climbed up on the gunwale and inched around to the bow. Once we'd sidestepped the wheelhouse, the wind and rain was enough to blow you over.

Sonny motioned to Inez and screamed, "Get her down below."

I took hold of Inez but she shook her head. She wouldn't budge, she was looking down at the sailboat. It had wedged in bow first about amidships the first time it hit but was now yawing in the wind, shredding paint from the doctor's hull and ours. It was about 24 feet long and must have drifted a long way. The three of us went back to the wheelhouse. Sonny pulled up a section of carpet and an engine hatch and brought up the last of our lines. We untangled them into four neat coils. Sonny grimaced as he worked. He was exhausted. Steering in the storm had whipped him.

"Sore arms?" I asked.

"I can barely lift them," he replied with a voice of gravel.

He turned to Inez. He'd known her since she was a baby.

"I'd feél better if you'd stay inside." It was the only time I recall him speaking to her directly.

"Please, Sonny . . . "

"That's no weather for you to be out in," he said, as though speaking to a princess.

"She just wants to help," I heard myself say.

He snapped at me. "She could slip over."

"I'll rig her a safety line," I said.

"Damn it, don't take your eyes off her."

"I won't."

I snugged a bowline around her waist and could feel her hips under the slicker. She cracked a smile and I smiled and the three of us went back out. We went around the gunwale to the bow and Sonny climbed over the rail and down onto the deck of the sailboat. It took him quite a while. I threw the line at him three times before he could catch it in the wind and he tied his end to a cleat in the sailboat's stern. Inez and I crabwalked over the bow to the bulkhead and climbed up on the dock. I unwound some of the safety line from around Inez's waist and tied it to a piling. She made a face at me.

There was a commotion down at the far end of the dock. A rundown converted headboat full of hard-drinking hippies was breaking up against the dock and they were trying to get the girls off one by one. That end of the dock was pretty unprotected from the wind. The dockmaster was shouting and the boat was rolling broadside and slamming back down on the pilings. We'd seen her as we'd come in with half her paint peeled off and a few flimsy bumpers. She was rocking pretty good even then but the kids had the music up and the wine and beer flowing. They'd waved to us, laughing and dancing around on the bow but nobody was dancing now. I watched a girl jump to the dock and fall and heard another one scream. At the other end of the dock, near the office, four men were having an argument. They gestured this way and that in the docklight. There was other shouting, we heard it from all directions in the darkness, the frantic cries of successful, otherwise calm men. Wealthy boat owners used to being obeyed, whom the storm terrified tonight, pounding their extravagant yachts against one another.

Several docks across from us, an ambulance flashed up and turned around. The back door opened and shapes in raincoats set a stretcher up and started it down the dock. There was the sound of breaking ice on our dock and we saw the party boat lose most of her windows on a piling. There were more screams and flying glass. She rolled up on another swell and came down deeper on the piling. When she rocked back a good portion of her super-structure sheared off onto the dock. A wave like an ocean sea broke over the windward side of the dock, flooding us until the water drained from the planking. There was more shouting.

There was something wonderful about it, Inez knew it, too. I checked her safety line and took a turn of the sailboat line around the same piling. I hauled the sailboat line hard while Inez drew up the slack. I'd move the sailboat out a foot and she'd center the loop on the piling and hold it there. Sonny held the sailboat off the two hulls, mostly off *The Katherine*, the angle she was coming.

It was slow going and coarser hempy rope this last of the line Sonny produced from the bilge. My hands then, at that age, were the strongest they'd ever be but they hadn't been really dry all day and the rope hurt them. I hauled away, slipping so much that I pulled, braced against the piling. Another big sea crashed over the dock in the same place and I checked Inez's safety line a second time. A plastic garbage can from somewhere skipped down the dock and flew through the air like a bullet. There was more yelling from the party boat, she was going fast and they were worried about the dock. I didn't know what we'd do with the sail boat once we had it out. She'd take a beating against the bulk-head, there weren't enough tires left to tie her there or to raft her on the other side of the doctor's boat. She was in as little wind as she'd be in right where she was, but there wasn't an outside piling to hold her.

Sonny told me to come aboard and help hold her off. I secured the line and when the mast stopped whipping I slid down it like a fireman. I hated the decks of sailboats, there was never any room to move with booms, winches, and halyards going everywhere. Sonny went below, cursing the cramped ladderway. I saw his flashlight beam through the hatch and felt the deck rumble a few times. He was trying to start the engine. I looked over the stern and saw water popping from the exhaust but it wasn't steady. He came up half-grinning.

"Won't run," he shouted. "Probably water in the fuel by now"

"Did you want to go cruising," I yelled back.

"Yeah," he shouted. "About forty-five feet." He went forward and looked at the deck, then he worked his way back to me, shaking his head.

"That anchor won't hold by itself. Go get ours. We'll throw both hooks and set her to ride ahead of us and out from the bulkhead. I nodded and climbed back up. He was a hell of a skipper when he wanted to be.

Our anchor was secured to the deck of *The Katherine's* bow. I unbolted it and started pulling up anchor line from the little hold down behind the bowstem. It was beautiful line, never used, and I knew it broke Sonny's heart to waste it on the sailboat. I pulled up about 200 feet and tied it to the bow cleat. I looked at Sonny who was nodding, we would need all that line.

I swung the anchor up to the dock, climbed up, and went to Inez.

She grinned at me.

"You're wet as a duck," I shouted. "Are you all right?"

"Yes."

"There's nothing to hold her off us so we have to use the anchor. Can you let slack out easy when we start to center her.?"

She nodded. "I think so."

"Just let line slip around the piling," I yelled in the wind. "If it feels like it's going too fast and you can't hold it, let go and don't worry about it."

"Okay," she mouthed the words in the howl.

"Let the piling do the work and for God's sake don't wrap the line around your hands."

"You're so adorable," she yelled. "Stop worrying about me and fix the sailboat."

I checked her safety line a last time and lowered the anchor down to Sonny. Keeping the length of line back to *The Katherine* free, I climbed down and met him on the bow. He had the sailboat's anchor rigged and ready to throw. It was about half the size of *The Katherine's*.

He shouted, "We should only have to do this three times," and motioned to the big anchor. "You're younger'n me."

I hefted the anchor up and over the bowrail and leaned as far as I would be stable.

"Heave it far as you can," he yelled.

I swung it back and forth below me a few times, letting out line. Then I drew back and slung it. The anchor sailed out against the driving rain, the line following it.

"That's the ticket, boy," Sonny shouted, pulling in line until it caught.

"Bottom," he shouted. We both took hold and I motioned to Inez to give us slack.

Pulling that line was murder against the current which ran like rapids. We got about eight feet before the anchor line was at too steep an angle.

"Throw the other one," he shouted.

I got the little sailboat anchor swinging and flung it a good thirty feet. It finally caught and we brought in enough line to pull the big anchor loose. I had the big anchor ready to throw again when the boat shifted. It was the sailboat anchor slipping and we shot toward the bulkhead.

"Look out," I screamed to Inez, dropping the anchor on the deck and running to hold us off. I was afraid the mast would hit her but she smoothly stepped back from the piling. Sonny ran to join me, cursing nonstop. When we were steady, I threw the big anchor again and we started pulling the bow around.

"That little sonofabitching anchor won't hold bottom," Sonny shouted.

"We pulled it too far," I said. "We'll only use it to get the big anchor up." I threw the sailboat anchor again, farther than the first time. I wanted as little angle as possible bringing it in. It caught and twelve feet of nervous pulling got us to the big anchor. I wound up and heaved *The Katherine's* anchor a last time at a quartering angle to the port bow and it caught in the good mud of the bottom, farthest out.

Sonny and I pulled the sailboat the rest of the way around and Inez fed us line until she was riding straight like the point boat in a "V" formation with the doctor's boat and *The Katherine* behind her. We cleated her and threw the sailboat anchor alongside the big one for insurance. We were fifteen feet from the bulkhead and a good twenty from either boat's bow.

The rain started to taper off. The dockmaster had come down to watch with four other men and they stood near Inez. When we secured the last stern line they started clapping.

The dockmaster shouted, "How are you going to get off?"

Sonny and I looked at each other. We'd been so intent on centering the sailboat we hadn't noticed we were too far from the bulkhead to jump off.

"Wait a bit," the dockmaster told us and turned to two of the men. The two headed off to another dock and came back struggling with a little fiberglass dingy in the wind. They dropped it into the current and heaved me the painter. When I had it alongside the sailboat we climbed down and stood in it, going hand over hand the bowline to the bulkhead.

"Where did you find the sailboat?" the dockmaster asked me.

"Adrift, between us," I said.

"You squared her away nice," he said, nodding at Sonny and then said, "one hell of a night." They pulled the dingy out of the water, then he and the others headed back down to the end of the dock where a Coast Guard cutter was towing the demolished party boat from the dock. The party kids ambled by with some of the girls wrapped in blankets. One girl was limping while another held a blanket around them both. The rain had stopped and we could tell they had been crying. We watched them hobble toward the marina office where a Coast Guard pickup truck waited with its lights on.

The sky behind the hills across the harbor was lightening. We watched it until we could see the tops of purple clouds above the hills swirling like seas. Sonny went below. Inez and I stayed until the light climbed above the clouds and the hills were green. I touched her arm and we walked back to The Katherine and went aboard.

Sonny had gone to bed but Mrs. Hutchinson was up. We changed our damp clothes and had breakfast while the wheelhouse filled with light. Inez's eyes were tired but they were wonderfully clear and we finished our coffee and looked at each other.

"Why don't you two get some rest," Mrs. H. said, pouring herself another cup.

"Do you want to look at everything?" Inez asked me.

I nodded, "I want to see the harbor before the wind quits."

"We can see it from the lighthouse if they haven't torn it down. I climbed it the year we rented bicycles." She turned to her stepmother. "Remember."

"Yes, but be careful. The ladder was rusty then and might be weak."

"I'll test it with my weight, Mrs. Hutchinson," I said.

"I'll get a sweater," Inez said and went below.

My sneakers were still too soaked to put on but it didn't matter. My feet in those days were tough and calloused from going barefoot all the time.

I checked the sailboat and the lines on *The Katherine* while I waited for Inez. She came out to the cockpit with her mother and I pulled the stern line to bring the boat close to the dock.

"I'll worry about you on that ladder," Mrs. Hutchinson said, watching Inez climb off.

"I'll take care of her," I said and we started up the dock.

The row of boats along the bulkhead were the most protected from the storm but nearly all had been damaged. There were cracked windows and gouges in the hull planking from hitting the dock. Radio antennas had broken in the wind, bridge covers, bimini tops had pulled loose from their fittings, we saw one floating near the bulkhead along with cardboard boxes, plastic cushions, charts, raingear and other stuff. The water was muddy and still churning with the wind and wild current. Even among boats that hadn't hit the dock the lines had chafed or worn furrows in the decks and transoms. Sonny and I had wrapped towels where *The Katherine's* lines could rub, which had helped but mainly she was built better. There was no wood like teak or that Honduras mahogany in a boat.

We walked past the marina office to the paved road that ran through the grassy hills to the beach. It was still early and only a few cars passed us. Inez found the dirt road that went up the hill to the light. It was steep and the sun was bright and we walked it slowly.

The lighthouse had once been painted white with red stripes but for years was faded and rust stained and overgrown at the base with the scrubby grass that grew on the island. The door had been removed so not to trap a summer tourist. I went in and tested the ladder. I climbed halfway up, where it was dark, and shifted my weight around, trying to break the ladder loose. It was solid and I went the rest of the way up to the deck that was light as day from the sun pouring in through the old windows. Inez came up slowly, her hands were as sore as mine from the night before and the rusted rungs of the ladder hurt her so much she had to stop several times.

The rain had washed the windows clean and we stood by them, looking at the island and the sky. The high, fast clouds from earlier, had disappeared and the hills were freshly green with white houses on the sides and a richer green in the folds. The wind was starting to die but still whined and hit the windows in gusts. There were whitecaps in most of the harbor and every part of it ran rough and muddy. Sailboats, outboards and anything light had washed up on the rocky beaches at the north end, the storm had pushed them up and the tide had left them there and the beach gravel shined like yellow jewels in the sunlight.

In the harbor, two white hulled Coast Guard cutters, a twenty-eight and forty-three footer, ran back and forth, towing everything that had lost its anchor and run aground. We were high enough to see the ocean beyond the tops of the hills. It was rough and dark blue and all the way out it was jagged below the line of sky. There were no boats on the ocean, none at all.

Looking at it, Inez said, "Can you imagine how it must be?"

"It must be unbelievable offshore. I'd like to see it, but I wouldn't want to be on it."

Behind us, on the road to town, there were toppled trees and brush and in town some of the streets were flooded. A small truck made a wake down one street and we saw a few people out walking in the part of town up on the hill. Then we looked at the harbor again and the sea. I was standing a little behind and next to Inez. The sun was higher and warm through the windows and on the deck.

I touched her arms and her shoulders and she looked down at the closest part of the harbor. I didn't think anyone had touched her that way before. She turned halfway and looked at me and kissed me once and I stepped us back against the counter the lighthousekeepers had used for their log, pulling her side to me. Both my arms were around her and she was looking down again.

I felt her side and the side of her breast, gently but deliberately, half expecting her to take my hand away, but she put her head to my shoulder as though she would fall asleep. I could smell the storm in her hair. I took hold of it and loved it and let it loose and found her shoulder and brought her a touch closer.

She lifted her head and looked at me. Her eyes were tired and I saw that thing in them I loved, and it made me want to weep. I was tired, too, tired enough to have wept, but not with sorrow and we started to kiss again and our mouths opened. I felt her hands on me, a woman's hands, and my back and shoulders strong and we kissed until we were out of breath. I held my face against her neck with my eyes shut and she trembled.

We were like that a long time. Then, and again, later, after we'd dressed, too shy to look at each other, I held Inez against me with the sky in the lighthouse windows and the harbor full of whitecaps and the mournful sound of the wind.

CHAPTER IV

It was years before I saw her again. I went to college that fall and Pete died in the spring. I came home at the end of the summer to look around before it was time to leave for the Navy. *The Katherine* was gone. Someone on the dock told me she was up north, probably at Cape Cod, and that everyone was on her.

Pete's brother was up from North Carolina, trying to sell the boat. I explained who I was and he told me to take something, anything I wanted, off her before he turned her over to the yacht broker. I asked for Pete's old set of fishing pliers. I showed him where they were and he gave them to me in their worn leather sheath and I shook hands with him.

In September, I left for boot camp at The Great Lakes. Twelve weeks later I was sent to The Helicopter Systems School in Memphis. That six months was the best time I spent in the service. The training fascinated me and disconnected me completely from the past. I liked almost everyone in my class. They were ordinary nuts and bolts kids, mostly from rural parts of the country, and we raised the standard hell of all young sailors in Memphis.

I'd requested sea duty and was assigned it—to a CH-46 squadron aboard The Appalachia, a small carrier modified to handle the big twin-rotored helicopters. I caught her in San Diego and saw what I could of the coast before we went to sea. It was strange being on so big a ship after the years of smaller boats. You rode so high and the motion was slower. We spent most days working on the aircraft and I qualified as a door gunner. Sundays, the ship's company would sunbathe on the flight deck and we'd crank everything up and give them a little show, climbing, autorotating down, and shooting up the water a few hundred meters behind the stern.

Our mail caught up with us in the Philippines and I learned Inez was engaged in a letter from my sister. We left Subic Bay for the South China Sea, the Appalachia's area of operations. Once off Vietnam, I was too busy to think of Inez or anything else. The piers were jammed at Cam Rahn Bay and we flew cargo off freighters anchored in the harbor. In the third month they ordered us to a tactical position off the coast farther north and everything changed. We worked almost exclusively with the South Vietnamese units operating in the mountains near the coast. Things were hot in the mountains that year and we flew medivacs around the clock. There was a battleship in our area, we couldn't always see her, but we could hear her all the time, especially at night when she lit the sky like lightening, firing into the hills and the lowlands beyond the beach.

We picked up wounded kids and flew them to the emergency clinic on board or all the way to the hospital ships in Cam Rahn Bay. Except for my R&R in Hong Kong and repair trips to the Philippines, I spent most of 1971 on The Appalachia. In my squadron alone we lost seven aircraft and twelve men. We steamed into Subic Bay Christmas week with three-quarters of the flight line inoperable and they pulled us off and kept us there. One month later, about forty of us caught a C-130 for Okinawa and, from there, a 707. The bird stopped once in Japan. It was an hour layover in the late afternoon and they told us we could get off and go to The Red Cross Welcome Station, but I don't remember anyone moving from those seats. I don't even remember anyone speaking again until we were lifting off that runway, headed for home.

But there was nothing for me at home. For reasons I would not understand for years, I couldn't bear family, friends, or anything else I'd known before. I thought I would find comfort or something in familiar places, but they depressed me even more. I felt like a very tense intruder from another time which, of course, I was.

It was a bad year, that first one back. I took a few hack jobs driving a truck and loading freight. I had absolutely no interest in going back to school. I spent most of my free time looking for new places to get drunk and pick up useless women who were equally drunk. As grim as things had been overseas, I had always looked forward to coming home. Now there was nothing to look forward to. I was a little screwed up. I had a touch of what later became referred to as environmental syndrome which tended to race my heart and caused me to sweat at inconvenient times. That and a healthy dose of survivor guilt. Also, for the first time, I saw where I was headed socioeconomically. I was headed nowhere.

Yet, I wanted. Maybe Inez wasn't completely out of it. My sister had seen little of her since the wedding. Those people drank, Ann told me, in a sporting kind of way. I didn't bother to tell her it sounded a notch or two above the way I drank. I drove by the Hutchinson's big beach house a dozen times, but had no business stopping in. I was too much of a wreck to face her, anyway. One aimless night, driving home, I realized that nothing much would change if my car went over the rail of the canal bridge. I slowed down and looked longingly at the dark current below the rails. Something had to give.

My sister worked for a fashion designer in New York. I hadn't known or cared much about New York, but I went up one weekend for a visit and change of scenery.

New York amazed me. Ann took me around and I enjoyed myself to the point of mild shock. I even stayed sober the entire weekend. That did it for me. I garaged my car at my mother's place and scraped up enough to find a rat hole near Columbia. I jumped at the first job I could get, selling industrial cleaners. Along with part of Brooklyn, my territory was the financial district—Wall Street.

It was as though I had stumbled on Fort Knox. Stockbrokers strutted those streets like tom turkeys. I met a few a year or two older than me, earning what seemed out of this world. Now, I wanted, hard.

I took a few finance courses at NYU under the G.I. Bill and began knocking on doors. Before I could take the securities exam I had to be sponsored by a brokerage firm. I knocked an entire spring and summer, starting with the bigger outfits and working down. Finally, I walked in on an old guy running a three man shop. He was a lean, tough-looking little bastard with round glasses and nicotine-stained hands. On the wall above his desk was a faded photograph of a P-40 fighter. Across the nose and intake were painted teeth and eyes, the unmistakable markings of Channault's Group—The Flying Tigers.

His name was Cyrus Foley and he had a hawkish look I'd seen in the faces of maybe five or six pilots I'd remembered overseas. But he grinned, looking at my service record and meager resume.

"Tell me who you are and what you want with me."

In five months of facing every conceivable interview technique, from being hamstrung by banker types who looked like furniture to the thirty-year-old hotshots who glanced away from you when they spoke, no one had put it to me that way. I looked at the plane in the picture, at the little Japanese flags painted below the canopy, and at the thin young man standing on the wing.

I cleared my throat. "I had just about everything once, I think. But I lost it a long time ago and now I want it back."

"You mean money or something else."

"Money and something else."

He shut my folder and nodded slowly.

"Well, if you make it, you'll make money. Maybe, for the first few years, not as much as in some firms. But I'll guarantee you this, you'll know a lot more than any of those other haircuts and, by then, it'll be up to you what you do with it."

I was too nervous to speak. It sounded like he wanted me.

"But remember this," he said, going even more hawklike, "this is a clean shop. We do the right thing here. Do you understand me?"

"Yes, sir."

"Good. And you can be sure I'll work your ass off. That means you're hired. Go pass your exam and I'll give you a spot here."

"Thank you, sir."

He stuck out a hand. "Call me Cy. And now go meet the other boys."

The other boys, who were well past sixty, labored from behind their desks and greeted me. Then I filled out forms for an hour, shook hands with Cy again, and burst back out to the street.

The afternoon was thick and hot and I walked all the way uptown, saving the subway fare, happy and sweatsoaked.

Cy hadn't been kidding, he did work my ass off. Nothing was easy with him, nothing beyond reproach. He took the first opportunity when I failed the exam.

"Did you study for the goddamn thing?"

"Yes."

"What happened then?"

"I'm just a lousy test taker, Cy."

"Is that the color horseshit I'll hear from you later?" "I'm just a lousy salesman, Cy. I'm just a this or that, Cy?"

"I screwed up the options part."

"That's better. That means you will correct it next time around. Every time you start thinking I'm just a this or that, you're throwing up your hands. We don't do that around here."

"Yes, sir."

"Now get somebody to drill you on options until you know 'em cold."

"Yes, Cy."

I passed on the next try. Cy took the second examination fee out of my draw which was skimpy to begin with. I never met a broker with a lower draw than mine. I asked Cy about it.

"You came in here with one year of lousy marks in college. That and you could take care of the company helicopter if we had one. I should have my head examined for giving you a draw in the first place. That draw is to keep you on your feet until you start earning commissions and no more. Nobody ever made it big on a draw. Now get on that telephone."

I prospected from eight in the morning until eight or nine at night. Cy took to the habit of fiddling around the office late, listening to each call and making comments. Then he would sit me down and spend a half hour explaining a particular security or area of the business. It was about the only time he let me ask him anything, as though I had to work all day before I was entitled to answers. Those late sessions were like buried treasure. As the weeks went by, I began to realize how knowledgeable of the industry he was and how proud of it. He wasn't about to give any of it away cheap. Later in my career, I met individuals who knew more about this part of the business and that, but nobody could ever put it all together like Cyrus. I ate what he fed me at the end of the day like a hungry dog.

I started opening a few accounts and the recommendations worked. Most were Cy's ideas from research contacts he'd acquired over the years. I built on small successes heeding Cy's admonition about taking short money, and always thought long term and big. Business owners, officers, and directors of public companies, retirees, all started giving me real money. Mr. Wentzel, one of the other brokers, retired and Cy turned some of his younger accounts over to me.

"Harry and me do better with the old farts," he said, smirking. He was strict and unbending with me as ever, but I knew he was delighted. He liked being right about hiring me better than he liked the business I was bringing in.

Two years passed like twin blurs, I was working all the time. It wasn't that I didn't want to do anything else, I just didn't have the energy. I was happy enough to spend my weekends sleeping. Even though I was playing a conservative game, I was starting to make more than I'd dreamed possible. I'd also acquired some self respect. By the spring of my third year, the combination of a favorable market, my spartan dedication, and Cy's hawk-like guidance allowed me to calm down a little.

"Look," he said with uncharacteristic fondness. I admire hell out of what you've done here, I've never seen anybody work half as hard. You'll make it. From here you want to start working smart instead of just hard. You've built yourself a base now leverage it. Don't work any more, do it by working less. Also, you're starting to look like hell. Take a vacation, get out of the city some on weekends. You don't have to work every single night."

I joined a fancy health club near the office and started to catch up culturally. I found a slightly less dumpy apartment on the East Side. When the weather was good, I took the train to my mother's for the weekend. Since I was just more or less passing through, being home didn't depress me anymore, although I still avoided bumping into anyone I knew. I did chores and garden work for my mother or went to the beach for a swim. On hot nights, I crashed on a cot on the porch. I spent a lot of time thinking about organizing my business. It was a pretty good summer.

One Sunday, after Labor Day, I stopped in the bar of a small hotel near the beach. It was an old casual place and popular with prep and Ivy League that summered nearby. I stood at the bar that day resolved to no more than a few—I wasn't drinking much by then. I was usually so bushed from work that liquor only made me sleepy.

It was late in the afternoon, and the bar was nearly empty. I liked the place. The wood of the bar where you stood, or sat on painted stools, was dark with age and the light green walls and duck murals were smoke-stained and peeling. There were wooden tables and chairs also painted and a few booths along the walls. There was sand on the painted concrete floor from barefoot patrons walking in and out all day. The breeze coming in through the screens from the ocean was sharp, it would be the first cool night of the year. I was talking to a man of about sixty in a blazer and tan slacks. He wore glasses with black rims and was a widower. His name was Frank Wolfington and he bought me a drink.

I thanked him and lifted my glass. We heard the door open and I saw Inez walk in with a heavy-set man in his thirties and another man and woman about the same age.

I spun and faced the bar again. I finished what was left in the glass and started on the one he bought me. I forced a smile.

"Cheers," I croaked, draining half of it.

"Picking up the tempo, I see," said Wolfington.

The place wasn't big. I didn't watch, but I knew they'd found a booth. I already hoped Inez was seated the opposite way so she wouldn't see me cross the floor to leave. Frank Wolfington was saying something to me. He had hardly touched his glass. I motioned to the bartender.

"Two scotches. Sorry."

"You're going to get me intoxicated before dinner. I asked if there was a good restaurant I could walk to."

"No. Folks drive into town for dinner, I think." I had to look, thinking I might have been wrong, that the woman I'd seen wasn't Inez. I faced Wolfington and strained out of the corner of my eye.

It was her, facing me. I took another bite of scotch and saw that her hair was different, straighter, it had calmed down. Her face had not changed, only tightened very slightly. She laughed at something the other woman said. The heavy set guy still stood. He turned and walked to the bar dressed in shorts and moccasins and a red polo shirt with the collar up. His head was large and he was heavy in the hips and gut, but not really bad looking. He moved well enough, but I could see that he wasn't comfortable standing. He bought four vodka and tonics, carried them to the booth and sat down next to Inez. Seated, he looked natural, then

I remember Ann telling me he was a lawyer. Suddenly, all four of them were looking at me and I heard Inez's voice for the first time in five years.

"Jim," she said.

I swore under my breath and turned to Wolfington who said, "You've been discovered, my friend."

"Will you excuse me a minute, Fred?"

"Frank. Surely."

"Sorry, Frank. I'll be right back."

It was a long walk, the twenty-five feet across the floor to their table.

"Hello, Inez." My voice sounded hoarse.

"Jimmy! How are you?" She was sitting between the wall and her husband. "You've lost weight."

I nodded, not really believing she was there in front of me. I wanted to go slow and not look in her eyes all at once, afraid something else might be there. I waited, then looked, finally, for the secret I'd lost. It was gone, knowing it had been there was just too much for me and I had to look away. She was saying something.

"Ann told me you came back looking terrible, but you look good, really, just thin."

"You spoke to Ann? When?"

"The last time? I can't remember? You've met Barry, no... "

The lawyer half stood and squeezed my hand beyond what was necessary for a friendly shake. He was strong, people who had never known much about it probably told him so, but his hand was flabby. He knew I could feel it when I squeezed back.

"Nice to meet you," he said. He was heavy in the neck and jaws.

"Nice meeting you."

Inez introduced me to the other two, Chip and Sally some-thing. Sally looked like one of those dopey girls in junior high that were always on the verge of giggling about something. Then I realized they had all been drinking, probably most of the after-noon.

I stood with my hands in the pockets of my shorts, looking at Inez.

"You're not still in the Navy, are you?" she asked.

Before I could answer, Barry said, "I played rugby against you guys at Georgetown."

I looked at him. "I don't think so . . . "

At the same time, Inez said, "No, Barry, not Navy. *The* Navy."

"Oh," he said. "I thought you went to Annapolis."

"No."

"You're out now, are you?"

"Yeah. I've been back almost four years."

Chip said to Barry, "My dad was a Navy Officer." And then to me, "Where were you stationed?"

"On float, mostly around Quang Tri."

It took a moment for them to realize what I was saying. And then I saw their faces change, all except Inez's. In those days, just mentioning Vietnam gave everyone an attack of either guilt or sanctimony, but they really got the creeps if they found out you'd actually been there.

Sally spoke first. "God, were you drafted?"

"No."

Barry was skeptical. "Wasn't the war over by then?"

"The ARVN's were still going at it."

They were quiet. I doubted they understood what I'd meant, but they didn't ask. Inez asked me what I was doing now.

"I work on Wall Street."

Barry shot like a bullet, "Which firm?"

I hesitated. I shouldn't have. "Eagle Securities," I said.

He shook his head and looked at Chip as though he had me.

Chip said to Barry, "Haven't seen the layouts, but I bet I could do something with that eagle." The two of them grinned at each other as if I weren't there.

Inez said, "Chip's in advertising."

"Oh," I said. "Right. We're real small. We don't advertise, but you can see our eagle in the phone book."

"Doing what?" Chip asked me.

"Swooping in for the nest egg." I looked at Inez who was a little tipsy and smiling at me.

Still looking at her, I said, "I haven't seen the boat in years."

"It's at the same place."

"And Sonny?"

"Same as ever."

"I'll have to go say hello."

"You really should, Jim."

Barry looked at Inez. He didn't like this talk. I knew he wasn't a fisherman and could probably care less about *The Katherine*, but had lay claim to her and Sonny as he had everything else.

"How does he know Sonny?" he asked Inez.

Inez must have sensed it and become frightened or something because what she said then established things in a way I wouldn't have dreamed.

"Jim worked on our boat, " she told everyone. Then she looked at the table.

I had no desire to speak, or to know what I looked like just then. Sometime later there was a hand on my shoulder. Wolfington stood alongside me. He addressed everyone.

"Pardon me. I just wanted to say goodnight to this fellow. I'm on my way out."

My voice cracked. "I'll go with you." I shook hands with Chip and Sally and Barry and then Inez without looking at her.

"I'll see you," I said, following Wolfington and waving blindly behind me.

Outside, it was getting dark and we walked the sidewalk to the row of high hedges and crossed the street.

"Will you join me for dinner?"

"No, thanks," I said. "I'm going back to New York."

We walked and he said, "Something tells me you were a little sweet on one of the girls in that foursome."

We stopped at my car.

"Yeah," I said, getting my keys out. "The one with the dark hair and dark eyes, sitting next to the fat-assed lawyer she married."

"Poor boy," Wolfington said and shook my hand. He turned and walked toward his car and I heard him say it again in the dark.

I went back to New York boiling. It was different now. I went harder than ever to do business. One late summer afternoon had robbed me of what I struggled to build with Cy. There was only money now and the questions how large and how fast to cure me from antagonists in casual clothes, including the one in shorts who had what was left of Inez. I went wide open.

My earnings exploded that fall. It only made me miserable. I was tense all the time about keeping it up and argued continuously with Cy. Just before the holidays, he opened a client's letter addressed to me (a New York Stock Exchange requirement for a principal), read it, and stapled it shut. I had no fuse left by then and went off like a rocket. He'd had it with me, too, for some time, and threw me out.

It only took me two days to find a spot with a big exchange member firm that wouldn't talk to me when I was a rookie. The industry was doing well and the place was typically overdone with departments, management layers, and secretaries all generating more paperwork than the Pentagon, trying to justify each other. The markets were good and I was simply a commodity. I swung my clients over with ease and went back into action. My production was excellent. Branch managers and regional vice presidents whom I'd never met, sent me notes of good cheer. It all made me more miserable. I had actually decided to crawl back to Cy when I heard he suffered a mild stroke and was selling his interest to the other partners.

A year passed and I took a look at myself and didn't care for what I saw. For one thing, I was completely alone. There was a hardness about me that eventually put people off. I had few friends on the job, none really. I had nothing even resembling a girlfriend. Dating women my own age was out. The smarter ones were going somewhere and they wanted someone like them along for the ride. I was introduced to a few through clients and the poor things would listen to me and look deep in my eyes and realize I was older than their parents. It was pretty hopeless. Paydays I'd get myself a hooker and then dinner alone somewhere.

I was back on that same desert island as after the war, with nowhere to go and no ships in sight. I went to Europe for ten days which broke things up, but didn't really help. In the spring, when the weather improved, I took long walks at lunchtime through Battery Park and up FDR Drive.

That was when I saw the boat coming up the channel, on the clearest day of the year. A March wind was blowing and her hull was white as a cloud.

CHAPTER V

Michael and I carried the bait down the narrow limestone road to the ice house. It was next to the little power plant, far enough from the club so the hum of the diesel-driven generators were out of earshot. We stowed the bait and walked back, sweating, the crickets noisy in heat of the scrub beyond the road.

When we got back to the room, Ciro wasn't there. We walked to the commissary, bought sodas, and poked around the shelves. Then we went back outside to look at the boats. It was all new to Michael. He knew a little seamanship, as much about sailing as anyone does, but the sportfishing universe was private and difficult to understand from the outside. I started showing him things—outriggers, fighting chairs, transom doors—the odd accoutrement found nowhere else. When you knew how utilitarian they were, how single-minded in design, a well-built fishing boat had a style as graceful as any schooner.

Michael listened to me, looking at the lone, barber-like chairs of stainless steel and mahogany set mid-deck.

"This part," he said nodding his head toward the chairs, "seems so roomy compared to the rest of the boat. Is that the after-deck or what?"

"That's the cockpit. It's where you fight the fish from. Can't have any clutter there."

He pointed to the wheel and controls mounted at the head of the cockpit, just inside the wheelhouse.

"How can you see in front of the boat from there?"

"The boat's run from the bridge. Those controls are for when you have a fish on and you still need the engines and rudders to position the boat, but have to be near enough the action to see and help bring the fish aboard."

"So you wouldn't normally drive the boat from there?"

"Run a boat, Mike," I told him gently. "You run a boat or steer a boat but never drive one. Yes, right, you normally wouldn't navigate the boat from there. Those cockpit controls are for the last part of the fight."

"Serious cool. How many people does it take to do all this?"

"Two who know what they're doing and the guy fighting the fish. The captain, the mate, and the angler."

"Will our guy have a mate?"

"Yup, me."

"Aren't you going to fish, too?"

"I doubt it."

"Why not?"

"Well, mainly because I know more than most guys he'd hire and we'll save a few bucks. Really, the thrill's the same for me if just I rig the baits and help you guys."

"Don't you want a chance to win the tournament?"

"Mike, we'll all stand a better chance of putting a fish in the boat if I work the cockpit."

We walked the length of the marina. There were some beautiful boats in for the tournament. They were still coming in, yellow quarantine flags up, from Bimini and the mainland. They topped off at the fuel pumps and the dockmaster assigned them slips.

Two Bahamian customs officials in white shirts and khaki shorts boarded each one before the yellow flags could come down.

"When's our boat coming?" Mike asked me.

"Not 'til later. He had a charter today and then its a two hour run from Nassau. I doubt we'll see him before dark."

I'd been edging closer to *The Katherine*. The slips were full on both sides of her with what I figured were regular boats at Little Cay. It was the length of dock most protected from the surge of the harbor as well as the most private. The slips were wide, easy as cake to back into. They wouldn't rent one of those slips to a charter boat, especially a Bahamian one like we were hiring and I was glad for that.

"Michael followed me to *The Katherine* and we stood looking at her.

"This is the one you asked me about."

I nodded, "I used to know her."

"It's a beauty of a boat. What make is it?

"A Rybovitch. All forty-two feet of her. What do you think of the hull shape?"

"Neat. She brand new?"

"She's at least twenty years old."

"I don't believe it."

"That hull became the basic design for about half the other boatmakers. You'll never see a Rybovitch that doesn't look new. Less than a hundred have been built."

"Wow. You've been out on her?"

"Yes."

A Bahamian in blue shorts and a white tee shirt backed out of the wheelhouse holding two strands of dacron line. Michael asked me what he was doing.

"Checking the splice. You can double the first sixty feet or so of line to make it stronger if the tournament allows it. That looks like new 80 lb. line. Double it and you've got a breaking strength of 160 lb. You can catch a mighty big fish on that if you play him right."

"I'm digging this," Michael said.

The Bahamian, obviously a local guy they hired, turned and looked at us. I asked him if the captain was around.

"You missed him," the Bahamian said. "He went into town to meet the owners."

"Who are the owners?"

"Don't know their names. I only fish with them when the boat's in here."

It occurred to me then that the boat might have been sold.

"Is the captain named Sonny?"

"Yeah, Mon."

"Is he a leathery looking bastard with a rough voice and a lot of time on the water?"

The Bahamian nodded, pulling out more line.

"Lotta time on the water. Lotta time in the barroom."

"That's him," I said.

We walked back to the club and around to the pool. The sun was behind the clubhouse and Ciro sat at a table on the shaded side of the pool. He was finishing a rum punch, saw us walk up, and ordered three more from a Bahamian girl in a flowered dress."

"Our ride hear yet?" he asked us.

"Negative, Admiral," I said. "But the bait is stowed and frozen. I'll pull half of it out tonight to rig when the ship shows."

"Can you rig it in the morning?"

"Yeah, but I'd like to get some started tonight.

"We've been checking out the other boats, Pop," Michael said.

The girl set the drinks down in front of us. I watched her tuck the tray up under her arm and walk back toward the bar with that island sway.

Ciro asked, "How, would you say, our competition looks."

"I'd say it looks formidable." I tasted the rum punch. It was delicious.

"And what, would you say, our chances are?"

"Well," I said, "let's think of it. If we don't get any weather, we've got a big enough boat. We haven't seen it yet or what shape the tackle's in, but our bait will be as good as anybody's. And we have this, most of these boats have just come over from the mainland but our guy's a local. He fishes these islands all the time and should know the waters better. So what really remains to be seen is how we'll all do together. Will we gripe and bitch and argue with each other? Will we lose our heads completely if we raise a big fish? Or will we and this captain, who's name, by the way, is Ulis, will we all sort of be good sports and have some fun and pull together like some kind of half-assed team?"

Ciro took a long drink, wiped his mouth and crooked an eyebrow at me.

"And what do you, as first mate of this expedition, plan to do if it all goes wrong?"

"What do you mean?"

"I mean, what if the weather turns nasty and the equipment's bad. What if our captain, who's name is Ulis, is that first or last, proves incompetent and we prove worse, and there are no fish in the ocean to speak of, and the three of us, in desperation and rage, reduced to remnants of the civilized men we were when we got here, finally turn on the captain and each other. Huh? What are you going to do then?"

"Yeah," Michael leaned forward. "What are you going to do then?"

"Stay so goddamn drunk I won't give a shit."

"Good. Let's not run out of booze then."

We had another round and the sun was getting low.

"One more thing," Ciro asked me.

"What's that?"

"Where can a guy get laid around here?"

"He can't."

"Let's definitely not run out of booze then."

"Anybody hungry," Michael asked.

"Everyone is," I said.

So, we finished our drinks, stood one by one and walked single file to dinner.

We had conch chowder and king mackerel, kingfish I'd always called it, fried, and broiled with salad and rolls. We had key lime pie and coffee. We split the check and went to the bar for a scotch. It was dark by then and the dock lights were on. We could see most of the little harbor. A few boats were still coming in, we saw their running lights a good way offshore and as each one came into the harbor I went out for a quick look but none was ours. We were at the bar a long time. I had four scotches and went outside to look again. I came back in and ordered a fifth.

"I don't know, guys."

"What time did he tell you he'd get in," Ciro asked me.

"I was really looking for him around seven or eight. It should only take him two hours from Nassau."

"It's quarter to ten," Michael said.

I knocked back the rest of the drink and said, "Mike, let's go put half that bait out to thaw."

We had a quick look at all the slips and stopped at the gas dock to see if we'd missed him, but they hadn't seen a thirty-eight foot Cubavitch come in. Michael and I made a mixture of baits in one box and carried it to the part of the dock in front of the bar. I took the lid off and we went back in. I figured Ciro had time for at least two since we'd left.

"Find our sled yet?"

I shook my head.

"He's got our deposit."

"Yup."

"Call him."

I went through my wallet for the scrap of paper with Ulis' phone number. I ordered a scotch and took it with me to the marina office. There was a pay phone there. When I finally made myself understood to the operator and got through feeding quarters into the phone, there was no answer. I walked back to the bar.

"He's on his way." I ordered another scotch.

"How do you know," asked Ciro.

"Where else would he be?"

"He and our deposit," Ciro said, "could be lost at sea."

Michael looked at his father and back at me.

"What if he doesn't show?" he asked. "What then?"

"What then," repeated Ciro.

I carried my drink outside and walked the marina quickly. I waved to the Bahamian at the gas dock and he shrugged his shoulders. I walked back to the bar.

Ciro and Michael looked at me.

"He's not there."

"We can sunbathe," Michael said. "We could snorkel. I could dig that."

"Nobody has to snorkel. We came here to fish. If he doesn't show we'll charter something else, even if it's a goddamn skiff."

Ciro ordered another round. I was getting drunk.

"I better wait outside." I took my drink out to the dock and leaned on the rail a while, looking at the harbor. I sipped the scotch but I had drunk so much that it had lost its taste and I emptied the glass in the water.

Through the inlet, about a half mile offshore, a set of running lights grew slowly. I walked to the gas dock, there was no one there now, and waited for the lights. What made the lights was too big, I knew, and eventually a huge, top heavy pleasure yacht came through the inlet like a floating suite of hotel rooms. I always wondered who the hell would want to plow around on such a thing. Obviously someone with money he didn't know what to do with. About all you did in a sled like that was live good and look at each other, and that you could do in town. The damn things rode so high that it was less like a boat than a building. I disliked anything that didn't work, boats especially. Fishing boats, carriers, even the few sailboats I'd been on, always paid their way, same as I had. But the cruising yachts were lazy. They were flashy and hollow and the clowns that owned them probably liked their women the same way.

I watched the yacht slow and the captain, who looked like a gigolo, made a great show of telling his deck hand what lines he wanted up first. I wouldn't be caught dead on a tub like that.

I took a walk down to *The Katherine*. Moths danced around the little cockpit light that was lit, but the wheelhouse and the small portholes below were dark. I walked back up toward the bar and saw Michael standing outside.

"This is for the birds," I said, yawning.

"Go turn in," he said. "I'll wait a while."

"I'm the one sleeping on the boat, remember?"

Michael took the key from his pocket. "Go stretch out in the room. If he doesn't show, I'll throw some blankets on the floor."

"You're not tired, Mike?"

"God no, I'm all revved up on this tournament jazz."

"Your dad still at the bar?"

Michael nodded. "Starting to check out the babes."

"Any in there?"

"Couple oldies."

"Okay, wait if you feel like it, but wake me up when you get sleepy and I'll crash on the floor."

"The deck you mean."

"Right."

"That's starboard, man."

"Screw you. Keep an eye on our bait."

"It's safer than its ever been."

I walked to the little cluster of one story rooms at the other end of the marina, found our number and opened the door. The room was warm and small with the light on. I opened my suitcase and laid out a pair of shorts and a T-shirt for the next day. I shaved and took a good hot shower, the water tasted slightly brackish. I dried off and put on a clean set of undershorts and opened both windows. The little curtains puffed out and the room cooled off.

I took my suitcase off the bed and got under the sheets. The boat wasn't going to show. I didn't know what we would be able to do about it in the morning, but I was tired, full of scotch, and too sleepy to think about it.

I went to sleep quickly, first down somewhere, and later it was a clear chilly day at the start of an Asian winter. I was walking toward an even metal noise, an old howling. Something dropped before me and I stood on the ramp of a CH-46, the colonel's bird, he turned from up forward and grinned at me. Andy was the crew, they'd gone down empty together that night, and on the benches along the bulkhead, in the yellow sunlight from the open hatches, sat my father, and Pete, and others. I felt the ramp go up behind me and the big machine lumbered sideways, that split second of uneven torque, and then up into the light and cold of altitude.

We climbed fast, higher than I'd ever been in a helicopter and, by the sun, I could tell the colonel had us headed south.

"As far as our fuel takes us," he told me above the roar.

We were running away. From terrible partings, from an end to things, and I flew with them in that brightness, the dead men, until the light and the howling faded and I was back in darkness, dreaming, the last one alive.

The door opened in the room and I had no idea where I was until I heard Ciro's voice.

"You awake, Jim?"

"Yeah." My mouth was foul from scotch and I squinted into the beam of the docklight behind him.

"Our guy's here."

"How do you know?"

"Because I've been drinking rum with him the last half hour."

"Does he have a slip?"

"Yup. Michael helped him get his lines on the pilings."

"Good." I got out of bed and threw on shorts and a T-shirt. What time is it, Ciro?"

"Twelve-thirty."

"I must have just missed him."

"Mike said he came in right after you left. He said you were bushed so we didn't wake you right away. The captain's starting to ask about making baits now so I figured to shake you."

"I was bushed but I'm awake now." I didn't bother to put on shoes and followed Ciro through the door toward the docks.

Halfway down the row of boats, I had my first look at *The Tina*. She was smaller and of harder construction than the boats next to her, but she sat lower in the water and was built better. Unlike the newer boats, she was all wood, no fiberglass, which made her a better sea boat, if duller looking in the docklights. Walking closer, I could see she was rough, her seams showed, she needed wood, and there were streaks of brown down her hull from the scuppers. Green fuzz grew all the way around her waterline and her bottom paint was faded, but that was all right, she was a work boat and fished pretty hard and there wasn't much time to haul her out and fuss with her.

Michael stood on the dock, grinning. He'd carried the bait up. I pulled a stern line and brought *The Tina* close. I hopped aboard and she was good and solid under my bare feet. I liked her.

There were coiled lines, an old cooler, and other stuff strewn about the cockpit in someone's idea of order. Dead center sat the fighting chair. There were two smaller ones sitting behind and on either side of it. I took hold of the big chair and tested it. It rattled and creaked when I turned it, but seemed like it would hold.

A tall black man of about fifty in a gray cap, khaki trousers, and a white T-shirt came up from below. He was holding a big adjustable wrench and his hands were wet.

"Problems, Cap?" I asked him, looking at the wrench.

"Na, just cleanin' the strainers."

"What I could see of his hair under the cap was gray and clipped short. He was lean but strong-looking and I remember thinking he must have really been strong when he was younger. He had a doubtful look in his eye, maybe about me, but I thought he looked straight enough.

"I'm Jim," I said. "The one who made the arrangements with you."

"Ulis," he said and we shook hands. "Sorry 'm late comin' over. Had an injector foul on me this afternoon."

"Did you get a chance to change it?"

"Cleaned it is all. She run right now."

"Great."

He looked at me.

"Got bait, Mon?"

"Mullet, bally, everything. Can I see the rods and reels?"

"Sure, I'll hand 'em out to you."

The wheelhouse was open to the cockpit, not much on privacy, but the best setup for fishing. There were no obstructions to the action. I liked that. Ulis went inside and unhooked the rods from the ceiling racks and passed them out. I set them in the holes in the gunwale that were actually rod holders, two to a side and inspected the reels. Ciro and Mike sat on the dock behind the boat, watching me.

"Twelve-O's with hundred pound."

"That okay?" Ciro asked.

I nodded. "I better start rigging bait. Can you guys hand down the box?"

"Here comes," Michael said.

Ulis came out with an armful of wire rolls, hooks, and pliers. He set everything on the fishbox in the stern.

"Hey Bones," he yelled to a tall thin Bahamian mate coming up the dock.

"Yah, Mon, goin' get 'um tomorrow, hey?" said the Bahamian, holding up a bottle of beer and never breaking stride as he passed.

I looked through the stuff.

"Is that stainless steel wire all you have?" I asked him.

"I always use it."

"I like the stiffer kind. It's easier to work. I'll try to bum some in the morning."

He shrugged and I opened the lid on the bait. It was good stuff. I took a big mackerel out.

"Do you have a big needle to sew the bellies?"

Ulis shook his head.

I flipped the mackerel back in the box. "We'll borrow one."

Ulis began uncoiling wire. "How long you want the leaders?"

"Fifteen feet."

"Long, Mon," he said, uncoiling.

I hoped he wasn't going to scrimp on us. "Need at least that much." He was used to kingfish, little white marlin, and sailfish. Those were the charters he had, greenhorns who thought a shark was a gamefish. Eight pound bonita on thirty pound line. An eight pound bonita was bait for what we were after. He'd better understand that.

I took a mullet from the box and used the tip of a hook to make a hole above the mouth. Then I pushed the hook shank up from the mullet's split bottom until the eye of the hook was in its mouth. I guided an end of wire through the hole I'd made, through the eye of the hook and out the bottom of the mullet's mouth. I looped the wire and used pliers to hold the loop while I twisted the ends, made three barrel loops and held the rigged bait up for Ciro and Michael to see. Ciro whistled, still drinking rum.

"First one I've tied in years." I kinked the leftover wire end and worked it back and forth until it broke. "You never want to use wire cutters on an end."

"Why not?" asked Mike.

"Doesn't clip it close enough. Leaves a sharp end that'll hang up on something or cut your hand. Kink it off and the end's smooth."

I ran my hand over the barrel rolls a few times to show him. Next, I rigged a ballyhoo which looked to them like a six-inch swordfish. I showed them how to curve the hook in so it came out halfway down the baitfish's underside. Then I fastened the hook shank to the base of the little bill and broke off the end.

"Why break off the bill?" Mike asked.

"Catches grass, weeds and stuff."

I rigged four more mullet and four ballyhoo. That gave us enough baits to get started. I went through the box and pulled a big squid from the bottom that was still frozen. I scooped a plastic bucket over the side and set the squid in the warm salt water.

"Mike, do me a favor. If the bar's still open ask them for a half dozen cocktail straws, the little plastic ones. Any color's good."

"Cocktail straws," he repeated. "Why not?"

Ulis looked at me like I was crazy. I loved it.

"Do you have any barrel weights? The little ones with holes through the center?"

"Ya, I think so." He went below and fiddled in a drawer and came back with a handful in different sizes and shapes. I picked the smallest ones from his hands like they were jewels.

Michael came back with at least fifty cocktail straws.

"I got a few extra," he said, setting them on the fish box with the other stuff.

I worked the big squid in the water until it was pliable in my hands. Then I laid it on the fish box and held the little barrel weight near its tip. I set a cocktail straw and a hook in line below the weight and figured where to cut the straw so they'd be the length I wanted. Ulis still had no idea what I was doing. I cut the straw then took an end of wire and pushed it through the very tip of the squid, back through the middle of the body and down near the eye. I pulled more wire through and threaded a weight on the wire and crimped it tight with pliers. I forced the weight and wire back up to the front tip of the squid until it could go no more.

"The weight keeps the tip of the squid in the water, trolls better." I threaded the cocktail straw on the wire and jammed it up against the back end of the weight.

"The straw keeps the weight and hook separated the right distance," I said, fastening a hook on the wire end. The barbed tip of the hook lined up exactly with the squid's head. I worked the hook in between the eyes and the whole apparatus was invisible. I held it up and Ulis' eyes were wide.

"You're a fucking magician," Ciro said.

"Only other guy could rig a squid like this was the one who taught me."

I only rigged one more like that. It was tricky. I messed up three times before I finally got the wire through. I showed Ciro and Mike how to release the drag on the reels and then we all had a beer to kind of toast things. I asked Ulis if there was an extra bunk below.

"You can have both V-bunks all the way forward."

"I'll sleep on board, then."

I followed Ciro and Michael back to the room and took a pillow and blanket. It was almost two o'clock.

"I won't wake you guys too early. It's not like we have a long way to run."

"How far do we go to fish?" Ciro asked.

"We'll probably put the lines out as soon as we clear the inlet. See you then."

I carried the stuff to the boat and went below, Ulis stood in the head, shaving. I passed him going forward.

"Might have to move some stuff around," he said.

I did. On both bunks there were old charts, life vests, rods without reels, dock bumpers, and sloppy coils of line. I stacked everything from the left bunk over to the right. I laid my pillow at the aft end and reached up and unscrewed the two small porthole covers and locked them open. I got up in the bunk and stretched out and pulled the blanket up over me. The cushions smelled of mildew and faintly of bilge, but the air coming in through the portholes was fresh.

I heard Ulis get in his bunk farther aft and the light went out.

"She's all boat, Ulis. Who'd you name her for?

His voice came back in the dark.

"My wife. She die, Mon."

I told him I was sorry. It was chilly, so I brought the blanket tight around me. My hands smelled fishy from the bait. Little ripples slapped the wood of the hull. It had been years since I'd heard that. I woke later when the current moved *The Tina* sideways. Twice it happened, an old fear of coming loose, but there was no storm and the lines brought her back.

CHAPTER VI

I woke at first light and heard Ulis cough. I dressed and went to the head and out to the cockpit to look at things. There was a slight breeze from the east and, in the light part of the sky, no clouds. I knocked on the gunwale for luck and pulled the outrigger halyards down to check the pins that would hold the line. They were just big old wooden clothespins, but they looked all right. Then I found a little file and sharpened about a dozen hooks. Ulis looked up from the galley and saw me. He started coffee and opened the engine hatches. While I was filing, he climbed down and fiddled around.

At quarter to six, I walked to the room and woke Ciro and Michael. While they were moaning I used the sink to wash my face and brush my teeth. We had breakfast in the coffee shop and bought some stuff in the commissary to make sandwiches. They bought beer and soda and I bought two gallon jugs of spring water. We all bought shirts that said, "Little Key Billfish Tournament."

As we were walking back to the boat a Cessna 310 came in low over the water. Just before the inlet, it climbed quickly to eight hundred feet, turned out over the trees near the beach and circled for the airstrip. We saw the landing gear go down then both engines went quiet and the plane disappeared below the trees.

It wasn't on the ground very long. We heard it idling fast again in a few minutes and then running up. The noise moved and as we reached the boat the empty plane arched above the trees and turned northwest, circled around the other side of the island and headed back to the mainland.

When we were aboard, the dockmaster walked up with one of his Bahamian helpers and gave us plastic number cards to put in the windows. We were boat number nineteen. Engines were starting up and down the dock.

"Ready now?" Ulis asked.

I nodded and he started the little diesels, one then the other. They warmed in a minute. I went up along the wheelhouse to the bow, untied a springline, and held it. I was barefoot and the engines felt smooth through the deck.

Ulis was on the bridge looking down behind him at Ciro and Michael who wrestled with the stern lines. While I was waiting, I looked down the dock. I was pretty high up and saw the red pickup stop behind *The Katherine*. The driver put down the tailgate and two men who had ridden in the back handed down their luggage. The other door to the cab opened and a woman got out. She was gray-headed and wearing sunglasses. Another, younger woman stepped out also wearing sunglasses. She was dark-haired and in her thirties. She watched the luggage come off and walked a few yards away from the truck. Then she turned and looked at *The Katherine* and in a moment I knew she was Inez.

"She was on the plane," I said out loud. I strained to recognize the men. I was pretty sure Mr. Hutchinson was the older of the two. The younger one was heavier, stouter. Barry. It looked like she was still married to him despite what my sister had told me.

I heard Ulis' voice.

"What are you waiting for?"

I was still holding the springline. I hung it on the piling, quickly untied the other lines and hung them. Ulis threw the clutches in and the engines idled down and we moved from the slip. When we were clear, he reversed the port engine and turned us. We had to go halfway down the dock toward *The Katherine* before we could cut around the outside row of slips to the inlet. I stayed on the bow watching Inez. The Bahamian on the boat the night before appeared and helped with their luggage. Then I saw Sonny climb the ladder to the bridge. He unsnapped the canvas cover, bundled it up and stowed it under the seats. When we were as close to *The Katherine* as we'd get, before we turned for the inlet, I yelled, "Sonny," and waved.

He shot around but didn't recognize me.

"It's Jim," I said and waved again.

He waved, but he still didn't know who I was. I just grinned and when I looked back at Inez, even at that distance, I saw her face change slowly around her sunglasses.

Ulis moved the throttles and we pushed through the inlet. He never brought us up to cruise, we slowed down a hundred yards beyond the rocks. He called down from the bridge.

"How many lines you want to fish?"

"Five," I said. "Four and a long one from the bridge."

I handed a rod up and he set the handle into the rod holder that was bolted to the side of the flying bridge. When he free spooled enough line down to me, I clipped the leader of one of the rigged squids and dropped it behind the boat. Ulis ran it out another eighty feet. The squid rode a little wild. I told Ulis and he slowed the boat a touch and the squid calmed down.

I climbed up alongside the wheelhouse to let the outriggers down. The brackets that held them in the down position had worked out and had been replaced with short lengths of nylon line. There was a lot of rope-tied, shimmied up, Rube Goldberg stuff on the boat. The radio antenna bracket had also broken and had been replaced with fishing line. Quite a few screws to things were backed out a quarter inch, obviously stripped where the wood had dry-rotted. Ulis had whittled down plugs and pushed them into the holes so the screws would have something to bite into. It took me a minute to figure the outriggers out. Once I did, I untied the nylon and eased both of them down. It looked half-assed but the lines held them at a proper angle. I slid back down into the cockpit and showed Ciro and Michael how to run the halyard down and clip the line to the pin.

"Keeps the lines spaced apart," I told them. I put a ballyhoo and a mullet on the outrigger lines and another each on the two flat lines. Then I climbed up on the bridge to get a good look at all five baits. The ballys and mullet were skipping like they were alive and all the way back, the squid towed smooth with a nice little wake.

Ulis asked me if the speed was good.

"Perfect, Cap."

There was only one seat on the bridge, the cheap plastic turnaround one Ulis was sitting in so I sat on the deck, looking back. We were headed southwest. Beyond the outrigger I could already see the low coast of Andros Island stretching out of sight to the south. I looked over the side at the bottom passing forty feet below us.

Behind us, boats plowed through the inlet and turned each to its own coarse which was usually around to the north. Ulis read my mind.

"We'll follow Andros down and zigzag back up in the after-noon."

"You're the skipper."

"Lot 'a ocean to cover. It's the right time 'o year."

I looked over the side again, but there was only deep blue.

"We're off the bank."

Ulis nodded. "Big hole. 'Bout a mile deep from here passed the end of Andros."

"But you like this west edge?"

He nodded again. "Anything comes down the channel ends up here."

"Any coffee left below?"

"Half a pot at least. I set it in the sink."

"Want me to bring you some?"

"Sure."

"How do you drink it?"

"In a cup, Mon, nothin' else. You want to steady that pot good while you heat it."

I climbed down and asked if anyone wanted coffee.

"Hell no," Ciro said. "I'm heating up nice for a beer."

I brought Michael below and showed him how to light the little propane stove. Ulis had wedged the coffee pot in the sink with towels. It was calm, but I held the pot to the stove while it heated. We filled three cups and Mike held two while I handed one up to Ulis. I leaned against the gunwale sipping the coffee. It was good to be in a boat again. I looked behind us. One boat with a hull like *The Katherine* turned west around the jetty, but I couldn't be sure.

There was a tremendous splash out beyond the outrigger. As we slid by it, I caught a large circle of green going down and the enormous green shape of a tail beneath the surface.

"Whoa," Michael said. "What was that?"

"A little whale," I said. "Went down the last minute. Probably heard us coming and waited to see what we were."

"Cool," Michael said.

I carried my cup up to the bridge and sat on the deck. A line of clouds moved in over the sun and the color of the sea changed. I watched the baits behind the clean gray swells of our wake. Two flying fish skipped away from us at an angle a few inches off the surface. I watched them fly level a hundred yards or so until I heard line stripping. One of the rods in the stern whipped and bent double.

"Fish," I yelled, starting down the ladder.

Ciro had been seated in the fighting chair, drinking a beer. He started to climb out toward the rod.

"Sit tight," I told him. I reached the rod, flipped the little lever to free spool and pulled it from the rod holder with line running out.

"I don't think it's a billfish," I said, but I let the line run out anyway. I counted ten, flipped the drag back on and hauled back on the rod. There wasn't much difference in the way the fish pulled. I walked the rod over to Ciro and set the butt in the gimbal of the fish chair and he took it.

I yelled to Ulis, "I think it's a bonita or something." He slowed the boat and Ciro settled down to fight the fish. Whatever it was, it ran in a zigzag pattern until he turned it and started taking in line. Ciro was rusty, his timing a little off, but he knew how to gain on a fish. He rested a couple times and I reminded him about keeping the rod tip up.

"Christ, I'm out of shape," he said. He'd broken a sweat even though the sun was now completely covered by clouds. When the leader came up there was a silver shine behind the boat.

"Barracuda," Ulis said.

I leaned over the transom, grabbed the wire and handlined it in. The barracuda came up teeth first, eyes glaring, crazy mackerel lines along his narrow metallic body. I flipped him up onto the fishbox, held him by the gills, and carefully worked the hook from his lower jaw. I held him up for Ciro.

"These teeth are like needles." I had him by the gills. When he and Michael had a good look I flipped it over the side.

"What the hell did you do that for," demanded Ciro.

"Junk fish. No good to eat. That one was too big to use as bait. We catch a smaller one and I'll rig him."

"Son of a bitch," Ciro said, climbing out of the chair. "I earned another beer."

Ulis speeded the boat back up and I put another mullet out.

I checked the drags on the reels and climbed up onto the port side of the wheelhouse with my arm around the ginpole. Standing there, I could see the baits almost as well as from the bridge and could be quicker to the cockpit. Two boats were in sight about a mile off.

I felt us turn. I looked around and up at Ulis who motioned with his head. Off the bow some Mother Carrie's chickens dove at the edge of a floating patch of yellow weed about the size of the boat. Ulis skirted the weed line and I strained to see the baits. There was a swell behind the starboard outrigger line and I heard the pin pop. A big bull dolphin flew end over end peeling line.

"FISH," I called, hopping down. Ciro was the closest and I handed him the rod and walked to the chair. Then the flat line popped and whipped and I knew we'd hooked the pair.

"That's the cow," I said to Ulis. He nodded, slowing the boat. I handed the flat line to Michael.

"Keep tension on that line," I said to him and then up to Ulis, "where's the gimbal?"

"In the hatch behind the chair."

"Hang on, Mike, and you can fight that fish on your feet.

I dug the strap with the little rod holder built into it. I buckled it around him and helped him get the rod butt in the holder.

"That's better," he said.

"'Lot better than trying to reel with the butt between your legs."

Mike giggled, struggling with the fish. "Cool, what is it?"

"Cow dolphin. Your old man's got the bull. A big one. Yours is the girl, prettier. They usually hit in pairs like that. There she jumps."

The little dolphin burst from the water like blue and yellow fire.

"Oh, wow," Mike cried, trying to get line. "This is great."

I ran into the wheelhouse and found a pair of cotton gloves in a tacklebox drawer. I ran back out and saw Ciro's fish make a strong run across the stern. I reeled in the other two lines and looked at Ulis who was grinning. Ciro's fish cut back inside like a rocket and the rod bent double.

"Jesus H.," Ciro said holding on. "This thing's a monster."

"He's got shoulders, that's for sure. Let him run himself out."

The lines were crossing. The fish could probably see each other and wanted to stay together. I grabbed Mike's rod and passed it under Ciro's and gave it back to him.

The female came up first, wild and shaking. I hauled the leader wire and flipped her into the cockpit. She hit the deck flipping and the hook came free. She flipped and sprung from the deck and almost flew back over the side.

"WHOA," Mike ducked, still holding the rod. I dove onto her and got her by the gills with both hands and stood. I opened the fishbox with my foot, slid her inside and shut the lid. I was taking the rod from Mike when the fish box lid banged up and opened and she was back on the deck. She flipped and flew out in an incredible arc over the side and was gone.

"WHAT!" Mike screamed.

"Sorry, Mike," I said. "She'll grow bigger." I heard Ulis laughing on the bridge and started to grin myself.

"OHHH," Mike groaned. "I don't believe it."

I turned Ciro's chair by the back, keeping him straight with his line. "Don't worry. We'll find more."

"That thing was beautiful," he said. "I thought a dolphin was a big smiling fish that did tricks."

"That's the mammal dolphin. Also called a porpoise. They're more like whales. These are fish with the same name. They're great to eat. Restaurants call them their Hawaiian name, Mai-Mai."

Ciro pumped the fish, gaining line. The dolphin was tired and fought back and forth slowly just beneath the surface. He came in at an angle like Michael's had, but with the power of a bigger male. I unhooked the gaff from where it hung beneath the gunwale and propped it, hook up, in the corner of the cockpit. I grabbed the leader when it came, and brought in the fish with short strokes. He jumped once to eye level with an angry look. I kept tension and hauled faster and he jumped again, soaking me. When he was alongside the boat, I took a turn around my hand with the leader and gaffed him with my free hand. He was heavy, I almost lost my grip before I let loose the leader and got my other hand on the gaff handle. It was all I could do to lift him over the gunwale. He jumped off the gaff, hit me hard in the chest and landed in the cockpit, thrashing and banging like he'd break the boat apart.

I dropped the gaff and yelled to Mike, "Open the fish box and hold the lid."

I knelt over the lovely mad fish and he flopped at me, hitting me in the face before I finally had his gills. The moment I had him clear of the deck, he thrashed a flurry. I got most of him over the box and let go and Mike slammed the lid and we both sat on it, looking at Ciro.

He still sat holding the rod in one hand and the slack length of leader wire in the other, sweat beaded on the shining top half of his head and a look of astonishment on his face.

I crossed my legs, the fish still hammering the box.

"Captain Ciro," I said above the banging. "You have just caught one hell of a dolphin."

"Yeah, Mon," Ulis yelled from the bridge. Now you cooking with something." He turned to rush the throttles back up.

I put baits out and Ulis found the weed line again. We made a few more passes at each side of it, but didn't raise a fish. There were no more birds around it, either.

The cloud cover around the sun had built to a high ceiling of solid gray and the breeze went down. I didn't think it would rain but the visibility dropped to a mile or so across the charcoal table-top of sea. We weren't far from Andros, but I never saw it again that day. I didn't see many boats either though some had to be fishing as far south as we were.

Ulis kept us on that coarse. We got into bonita. It started with a commotion of birds a long way off, working over a half-acre boil of water. Ulis brought us up easy and we saw school-sized bonita, individual fish, jumping after bait, swimming so tight you could walk on them.

We hit them every pass. I kept handing rods to Michael. He caught four and Ciro and I reeled in two apiece. We fought them all standing up. No one ate bonita unless they had to, I threw them all back, they were too big to rig, and we left the school, still slashing bait below the birds.

I rigged another squid and half-dozen mullet and ballyhoo for the baits we'd used and climbed up to the bridge to spell Ulis.

"That was good, those bonita," I said. "Thanks for staying in them."

"Figgered the young one needed to catch some after the dolphin. He get his fill?"

I nodded.

"We got bait enough to stay in 'em as long as they want to, but it ain't findin' us billfish."

"I told them that. You did right, Cap."

"Hold her one-ninety. I'm going down to pee."

I took the wheel. She was hard steering, the linkage needed some grease but she responded well, better than any fishing boat I'd steered. I asked Ulis about it when he came back up.

"Got them big rudders, Mon. She turn like she should."

"They don't lose you any speed?"

"Some, when you hook up and run from island to island like last night, but I don't have to run much."

"I forgot that. You fish so close to shore you hardly ever run at cruise."

"Not much. I like to run her in at the end of the day. Clean 'er out." He pointed off the bow. "Look a' that, now."

I looked ahead of the boat but didn't see anything. Years in front of an electronic quote screen hadn't done much for my eyesight.

"I don't see anything."

"Wait, Mon. He be back."

Up out of the gray then, a lighter shape of gray came up steady and broke, the smooth slippery back rolling evenly and the short curving dorsal that was nothing like a shark's. It rolled down and then I saw another back and several more. We were in a school of porpoises.

I went down to show Michael. Now there are your dolphins, the other kind."

A dozen swam with the boat. Alongside the wheelhouse, two jumped clear of the water with almost perfect symmetry.

"Oh, wow," Michael said.

"Having a look at us."

The same two went down and raced under the boat. They came up on the other side and jumped again, one behind the other.

Ciro was sitting in the fighting chair. "Look," he said, pointing behind the boat. There were porpoises following two of the baits. They swam up smelling the mullets and nudged at them.

"Should we reel in the lines," Ciro asked me.

"No need. They're just playing with em. They'd never hook themselves."

The tips of both rods bent slightly as they took the baits in their mouths and tugged gently.

"My God," Michael said. "It's amazing. It's like they're trained."

"Just unbelievably smart," I said. "They know those baits are rigged. They think we put them out there as toys."

I turned and looked at Ulis who shook his head. Mike saw it too and asked me what was wrong.

"We won't catch a thing while they're around."

"Really?"

"Billfish, sharks, everything knows to run from them. Big sharks may take a small one but no fish'll mess with a school."

Michael watched the porpoise tug the baits. "Then they're safe as long as they stay in groups?"

"Most of the time. Smart as they are though they can get cornered by killer whales. If there's enough whales to surround them they're in trouble. But mostly they don't have to run from anything."

The porpoises swam with us. Individuals became less shy, barreling alongside, half-rolling a few inches deep with wakes like torpedoes, swimming on their sides to see us better, faces fixed in that natural smile, rolling back and diving under the boat.

Ciro asked, "Can we outrun them?"

"Probably," I said. "At least they'd get tired of chasing us. Best way to lose them is to pass 'em along to another boat, but we're alone out here."

"They're so neat to watch," said Michael.

"Yes, they are."

We had sandwiches then and fruit and slices of cake that the marina packed. I spelled Ulis again at the wheel. Michael came up on the bridge with me and I let him steer for a while. One moment the porpoises were pushing along, rolling around us and the next moment, probably by some strange signal to each other, they disappeared. The ocean was empty again with little ground sea running, gray and unbroken.

Ulis came back up and I went down to check the baits. There wasn't a mark on any that had been tugged on. I showed them to Ciro and replaced them anyway. Sometimes the cloud cover broke and lighted cloud-sized patches of ocean a half mile distant, a shining silver-gray beyond the dark like the lighted end of the earth. We trolled that way for hours, toward the firey edges when they appeared but no nearer them, raising nothing, the arrows of our wake like a trail across lead.

The emptiness of the afternoon reminded me of my soul and I thought of Inez, suddenly, and admitted to myself I'd been thinking of her all day, since the afternoon before when I'd first seen *The Katherine*, and most of my life as well.

And now, what was simply a boy grown into a bitter man, there was no way for me not to love her. I'd lived on anger, partly because of her, but never at her, not even at the last time, not at the black, young-girl's hair or the sweet dark hurt of her eyes. That she had married changed nothing, as nothing I had done had. Losses, struggles, useless diversions, not the heat of whatever had come along. There was still Inez, only Inez. I loved her and it was so goddamned sad and hopeless that I wanted to weep. I stood with my head down, staring at the sad roll of ocean beyond the boat.

"The outrigger," Ulis said quickly.

The moment I looked up a thin bill scizzored through the water behind the outside bait and the line popped out of the clothespin.

"Fish," I said, heading for the rod.

Ciro was awake in the chair. I flipped the reel on freespool, took the rod from the holder, raised it over the flat line and helped him get the butt in the chair gimbal. Through Ciro's arms, I held my thumb on the turning spool so it wouldn't backlash.

"He's swimming with it," I said, still bent over him.

"What do I do?" He was holding the rod, watching the tip bounce with the mild pressure.

"Wait." I looked up at the bridge. Michael had climbed up and stood holding the bridge rail.

Ulis looked down at me, "Sailfish," he said.

"Hot damn," Ciro said, watching the reel roll.

"Get ready, boss. When I flip the drag, haul back smooth but hard. Set that hook in his mouth."

"Okay," he said, excitedly.

I flipped the little lever and the rod tip bowed and Ciro felt the fish. He strained back the rod.

"Put it to him, Ciro! That mouth's all bone!"

He hauled back again with his back and legs in it. The reel screeched and I turned to Ulis, making a fist and he slowed the boat.

Michael yelled from the bridge and Ciro and I saw the sail-fish jump backwards a hundred yards out, whipping his head side to side and flopping back with a splash.

"Whoooeee," Ciro giggled like a kid.

"I would say you hooked him, boss."

The rod bowed and line screamed off as the sailfish made a run like an arrow.

"Let him run, Ciro, but be ready to get line fast."

I reeled in the flat lines and the other outrigger. Michael brought in the bridge line and when the leader came over the transom, I set the squid in the cockpit out of the way.

Ulis called down to me, "What did he hit on?"

"Ballyhoo," I shouted back, "rigged with the magic touch." The rod tip went up.

"Get in line, Ciro," I said and he reeled like a madman.

"He's swimming toward us," Ciro said, working.

"At us at an angle. I can see the line cut water. Reel, man."

Ciro got a good forty yards until the sailfish turned and ran back out. He jumped broadside, quartering away, probably to see what had him, and we saw him again in slow motion against the drag of all the line through the water. He hung a full second, slightly bowed, in thin air as if already mounted.

"Whooaa . . . " Ciro and I said together.

"Jesus, Dad, did you see that?" asked Michael excitedly from the bridge.

"You're damn right I did."

I yelled up to Mike. "Got your camera up there?"

Michael shook his head.

I ran into the wheelhouse and found the camera and handed it up to him.

"Thanks, man."

"You'll get the best shots from up there."

The rod went straight and dead in Ciro's hands.

"What . . . did I lose him?"

"Reel! Reel!" I shouted.

Ciro wound in line, saying, "I think he's off . . . "

Then the rod bent double and we saw a sheet of spray and then the sail cut through the water, twisting, and went down.

Ciro held the rod tip up, expertly. It was a heavy reel for a sailfish. Line stripped out and the fish tired rather suddenly. I watched the reel spin in spurts and then it stopped.

"Pump him in boss," I said and Ciro started to reel, but very slowly. The sailfish didn't run like a sailfish anymore, but like a dead weight.

I turned to Ulis. "He's pulling like a shark."

Ulis nodded, watching the water behind the boat. "Are you gettin, line?"

"Yeah, but slow."

Ciro grimaced. "It's like I'm reeling in a bucket."

I tried to imagine what could make the fish pull so oddly. Ciro stopped, holding the rod tip up.

"Man, he feels like a ton."

"Go easy, boss," I said.

And then to Ulis, "We know he's not foul hooked."

Ulis shrugged his shoulders.

Ciro grunted, reeling again. He was a fighter, but out of shape. I knew he wouldn't quit the fish and I worried about him hurting himself. I'd give the fish to Michael if he got bad. It wasn't a tournament fish anyhow.

"Pace yourself, Ciro. He's not going anywhere."

"I'm getting line," he said, with much breath.

Then Ulis stood up, looking out beyond the stern.

"What?" I asked.

"He's coming in backwards," Ulis said.

"Yeah," Michael said. "There he is."

"What's going on?" Ciro asked, slowly pumping and reeling.

"It's around his tail," Ulis said and sat down.

"Shit," I said.

"What's the matter," Ciro asked me.

"He's got the leader wrapped around his tail. Probably swam through some slack when he ran toward us. It's not your fault. Those reels are geared low. Strong for a big fish, but they don't have a quick enough retrieve for a sailfish.

I looked up at Ulis. We both knew the fish was drowning.

I turned to Ciro. "You didn't want to mount him, did you?"

"I don't know."

"Think of the money you'll save." Then I looked at Ulis. "Back down on him."

"What for?"

"To get him fast. C'mon."

I put the cotton gloves on. Ulis stood and threw the engines out of gear and into reverse, I told Ciro to be ready to reel as fast as he could.

"It'll be easy now," I said.

The engines ground in reverse and the tension came off the rod. Ciro cranked like a demon, filling the reel.

Thirty yards out I saw the sailfish on his side, the leader running the length of his body and half-hitched around his tail. He rose slightly with a swell just below the surface, motionless as a log.

"Get him in, Ciro," I said.

The swivel came up and Ulis took the engines out of gear. I wired the sailfish in to his tail and eased him tail first into the boat. He was long but light and magnificently colored. I could hear the shutter of Michael's camera on the bridge. I cut the leader from his tail and worked the hook from his mouth with the pliers.

"Grab his tail, Ciro."

Ciro climbed out of the fighting chair. "What are you going to do?"

"Set him back in the water."

Ulis said from the bridge, "He drowned, Mon."

"Like hell. I saw his gills pump once when he was coming in."

We eased the sailfish over the side. Ciro let go the tail and I held him by the base of the bill, most of my gloved hand in his mouth. There was no pressure on my hand.

Ciro asked me what I was doing.

"Walking him."

The fish was buoyant but not breathing. After a minute, I hollered up to Ulis to put one engine in gear.

"Just idle her ahead. We need to get water moving over him."

Reflexively, the sailfish's tail waved in the current.

I held him and said to Ciro, "This ain't a tournament fish. We ought to release him if we can."

"He looks finished, Jim."

"Maybe not."

Very gently, I worked the fish's head side to side through the water. His gills hadn't moved and there was still no pressure on my hand. Watching his gills, I noticed the sailfish's eye.

On the bridge, I heard Ulis say to Michael, "Dot fish is dead."

I worked the fish evenly, watching the eye. It looked less dull and seemed to be staring at me. Through my glove I sensed a firmness, so indistinguishable that I supposed I was imagining it. The tail seemed different, too, it still moved with the speed of the boat but had acquired a certain tension. I spent a few long minutes doubting it and then I saw the gills flutter.

"He's on his way back," I said to Ciro. My arm was getting tired.

The gills started to move like a dying fish in reverse. He was silver shine of belly again and his back and sail began to throb with dark and light colors of blue. I held him, watching his eye grow wild. He started to quiver a bit around the head and I talked to him, holding him. He settled down and swam stronger, the wild eye looking at me.

"Is he actually swimming."

"Kind of. He's still weak, though." I turned to look up at Ulis. He grinned and shook his head.

"How far you gonna drag dot fish?"

"Til I can't hold him."

My arm was heavy as lead. The fish jerked his head once, splashing me and Ciro.

"Now he break your arm, he so grateful," Ulis said.

I called up, "Take a picture now, Mike."

"I already shot the whole roll."

The sailfish exploded then and my grip gave. He followed the boat a few seconds and then I watched him go down, his colors as bright in the clear water as when we'd first hooked him. He swam without fear to about twenty feet then turned and raced away like a bullet.

I slapped Ciro on the back. "Congratulations, boss. One hook and one release.

"I took eighteen pictures," Michael yelled from the bridge.

"What a hell of a gorgeous-looking fish," said Ciro, beaming.

I yelled up to Ulis, "Where's the goddamn release flag?"

He looked down at us and said, "I been meanin' to get one..."

"Awww," Ciro groaned. "What kind of fucking captain doesn't have a release flag?"

"The kind that never releases fish," I said, putting the squid back out and then up to Ulis, "You got anything red on board, a hunk of red rag or something?"

Ulis shrugged. "You can look around down below."

Ciro followed me below, thinking the same thing. I led him forward. There was a canvas bag on Ulis' bunk. We shook the contents out on the bunk and stuffed them back in the bag. Ciro opened the closet. It was filled with old charts and other mildewed stuff. He shuffled everything around and slammed the door.

In one of the drawers we found a burgundy wool shirt. Ciro unfolded it.

It's probably the only warm shirt he owns," I said.

"That makes it all the better."

Out in the cockpit Ciro held up the shirt and I found the sharpest fillet knife. I made a big show of starting to cut.

"That's my good shirt, Mon," said Ulis from the bridge.

"We won't need much of it," said Ciro.

I made two slits down the back and hacked a rectangle of cloth loose. Ciro held the shirt, turning it. He gestured the empty back panel to Ulis.

"You're fine, just wear a jacket."

Ulis shook his head, swearing, but I could see he was about to grin. He faced the bow then turned to the side and called down to me.

"Reel in the fucking lines, it's almost five o'clock."

Mike brought in the squid and Ciro and I the other baits. The last leaders came up and Ulis pushed the throttles slowly up to cruise. Carbon from nine hours at idle poured out and a diesel cloud hung over the water like a marker where we'd hooked up. I looked back at it, stripping the baits and dropping them in our wake. Out of nowhere, a shearwater dove down at the baits. He followed the boat, starting his dive each time my arm sent something over the transom and stayed with us a bit after the bait was gone.

We ran north almost an hour and the clouds began to break. There was wind now and a light chop. We'd trolled like a barge over glass all day and now Ciro and I ducked spray in the cockpit.

"She hops along," he said to me.

"She's a good little seaboat. It takes some wind to show it."

"I've been on forty-five footers that didn't seem as stable."

The water was clean and light blue again and, off the bow, we could see the Cay under a row of clouds. There were the rocks of the jetty and the low stretch of beach to the right. Other boats ran toward it, most across our bow, on the way in from Northwest Light. One fast one with a low hull like a Rybovitch was coming up and I felt the turning over in my chest and I climbed halfway to the bridge. I asked Ulis what frequency the tournament boats were on.

"Don't know, radio's out."

"When did you find that out?"

"'Bout a month. Dynamotor's bad. I been waiting on a new one."

I climbed back down and told Ciro over the engines that we had no ship-to-shore.

"I didn't think to ask him," I said.

"Be nice if we get stuck out here. From hunger, this guy is."

"We can fish Northwest Light tomorrow, if you want. At least there'll be other boats in sight."

"Fuckin' first class." He shook his head, but he was still excited about the sailfish and not much would bother him. He dug through his duffle bag and pulled up a bottle of Jack Daniels and gestured to me. I nodded. I never drank on a boat, but we were almost in and he'd caught his first sailfish. I opened the cooler and chopped enough clean ice to fill two plastic cups and handed the water jug and the cups full of ice to Ciro.

"Splash in yours?"

I nodded and watched him pour the whiskey to the motion of the boat. He added water to mine and handed it to me.

"Salute," he said and we each took a good pull and carried the drinks out to the cockpit.

Ulis was just easing up on the throttles and the inlet was coming up. We bounced into the chop of the mouth and then it was carpet-smooth, down out of the wind. There were birds on the jetty rocks above us, there was still plenty of daylight, and

Bahamian kids climbed out the jetty to fish the afternoon tide. The little ones waved and older boys watching them nodded to Ulis. A few small clouds still flew over the Cay, but mostly it was bright, a beautiful spring afternoon.

We were one of the last boats in. We tied up and I hosed down the rods and the cockpit while Ulis raised the hatches and looked at the engines, I showed Michael how to use the chamois and he wiped down the rods and hung them in the wheelhouse. Ciro made another Jack with water and stood on the dock, directing us. The tournament master, an elderly gent with white shorts and wobbly legs, worked his way down the dock for our report. We were given no credit for the sailfish, but Ciro described the action and release several times, his other fishing experiences, his construction business, and, finally, the last half of his life, pausing at intervals only long enough for Michael to make him and the tournament master drinks. I fussed around the cockpit, rigging a few baits for the morning, then Mike and Ulis and I had a beer. There wasn't any way not to drink around Ciro, some natural force he had made you want to jump right into the festivity. I sipped the beer grinning, finishing up a mullet and careful not to correct anything he said. The tournament master stayed around until the sun started to set. They gave what was left of that bottle a workout, Ulis pitching in. The sun was down when the tournament master finally shook hands with us and ambled back up the dock on rubber legs. Ciro was still mainly sober, but excited. He turned his drinking force on Ulis who'd come up with a bottle of rum. I nursed my third beer. It was going to be a long night.

Ulis filleted the dolphin and cut one in half and put the rest on ice. He took the half below and started the little propane stove. We told him we'd check on him later and asked him if he needed anything. He shook his head and sipped his drink and started to hum.

We walked back to the room. Ciro turned on the air conditioner and stripped to his shorts. He flopped back on his bed, stomach up, and covered his eyes with his forearm. In a few minutes his mouth opened and he began to snore. Michael had gone face down on the other bed and wasn't making a sound. I sat in the chair watching them until my head bobbed, then I threw the chair cushions on the floor and lay on them. The room rocked a few times and then I felt the sun I'd taken, a few old dreams came and went and then there was nothing.

A time later came another sunlight, the brightest I'd known, and the big hills beyond the coast, they were mountains really. I was climbing back over them to the coastal plain and then over the great haze of sea where the carrier sat thousands of feet below, gray and unmoving. We lost everything then and hung one heart-ending moment and the dirty white numbers and painted lines of the flight deck twisted below. Down we spiraled, like falling rock, so fast the rotors oversped, the sea and carrier coming up, and the wind so loud I couldn't hear my own curses.

And then I was on the floor with the shades drawn and the air conditioner going. It was the dark ceiling I was looking at and I lay blinking, covered with sweat, still cursing through a mouth dry from the beer.

I fell asleep a second time and then Michael was up and I heard him in the shower. Ciro's snoring had gone loud and regular, when the shower turned off I could hear him grinding away. I sat up and looked at Mike who was drying off in the bathroom light and grinning. He flicked on the room lights and Ciro choked in the middle of a snore and woke up. He coughed and rolled on his side and we heard him swallow.

He said in a husky voice, "I was damn near asleep there."

I stood up and threw the cushions back on the chair. "You were like a goddamn chain saw."

"How long were we under?"

"More than an hour," Mike said, pulling on clean under-wear. "Do I need a jacket?"

"Yeah," said Ciro, still on his side with his eyes closed.

"I didn't bring one."

"It's optional then," I said, stripping off my T-shirt. It was still damp with sweat.

"Wear one of mine," Ciro said.

I slid by Michael to the bathroom. My face was a little red in the mirror, but I could really feel it on my neck. I peed in the bowl and took a shower as hot as I could take it. When I toweled off, I felt good. Mike had left and came back as I was dressing. He'd gone after ice. We both had a light scotch while Ciro was in the bathroom. When he came out he had a towel wrapped around him like a skirt and the hair on the side of his head was up all crazy around the bald top. He was fat but firm and I thought he must have been a tough little bulldog when he was young.

He said, "It's customary to make a drink for the guy who's booze you're drinking."

"In these Bahamas," I explained, "you take care of your men. You catch a fish and you spring for the crew."

Mike swished what was left in his plastic cup and finished it. "That's us."

"I've sprang enough for you over the years." Ciro faced the mirror and started to brush his hair.

"Movie star," I said.

When he finished one side he turned and looked at me.

"Hey. You got a girl?"

I took a drink and played with the ice in my mouth. I held the cup to my mouth and dropped it in.

"No."

He faced the mirror again and started brushing the other side.

"Took you too long to say no."

I didn't say anything.

"Get yourself one," Ciro said.

"I'm too busy rigging baits."

"For who?"

"You and everybody else."

He ran the brush over a final time.

"Never has so little hair been led by so many brushings," said Michael.

Ciro slapped on some aftershave, "You're flagged, my boy, the fucking night."

"We might not run so far south tomorrow," I said, making myself another very light one. And then to Ciro, "what did the dockmaster tell you?"

"A few whites were caught, but only one blue marlin. They estimated it about one-fifty so they released it. I think he said it was around a light buoy."

"Northwest Light. It's small fish they're raising there." "Still, if you want one for your wall, we only have one day left."

"Could have used the sailfish for my wall."

"Shit, let's kill one fish and do it right," I said, "a tournament fish."

Michael asked, "So where do we find a tournament fish?"

"Around bait," I said. "A big fish is a loner. I can't remember raising a bunch of fish when I've caught a big fish. I think they drive the other ones off the bait. Only thing'll hang around a really big marlin is another big marlin, either a mate or one that'll respect his size and work the bait with him."

"We go to bait then." Ciro had buckled on a pair of chinos and took a clean shirt from the hanger.

"Right, but the bait might not be in the same place two days in a row. Even if the wind doesn't move it, all those boats could drive it down or out of there. The bait can't go west into The Bank, only northeast or south where we were."

Ciro buttoned the shirt. "Then Ulis was right to take us where he took us."

"Yeah, maybe a day early but the water's right and you did catch a nice sailfish."

"This ain't no sailfish tournament," said Michael, like an old salt.

"Listen to this guy. Okay, I might see someone I know at dinner. If I disappear, it's because I'm trying to get information."

"As in longitude and latitudes," said Michael.

"As is the loran numbers. If anybody raised or saw a keeper away from the fleet."

Ciro said, "Ulis doesn't have a loran."

"No sweat," I said. "All new nautical charts have loran numbers on them. We get the numbers, figure the wind'll move them some, and plot a coarse to the fish."

"Not bad, matie." Ciro pulled on a jacket. "Anybody hungry?"

"Aye, matie," said Michael.

"Fucking aye, matie," I said.

Ciro stuffed a few cigars in his jacket pocket. "Let's get, then."

We stopped by *The Tina*. It was dark now and in the docklight you couldn't see the brown streaks running from the scuppers along her hull or the patched dry rot on each side of the bridge. The lights were on the water like moon lights in the black of tide rushing by her hull. Walking up the dock we said nothing. We liked *The Tina's* shape, modern as any hull near her and more solid, and that it couldn't be noticed where she was rough.

Ulis was straightening up the galley. He heard us jump down into the cockpit and he grinned up from the galley light.

"All clean and shiny," he said, looking us over.

"How are we on bait?" Ciro asked.

I said, "We've a lot of baits yet and quite a few rigged up." I leaned down into the galleyway and said to Ulis, "I'm going to see what I can see tonight."

He nodded, sprinkling cleanser in the little sink in a slow, rhythmic motion. It was like there was a continuous singing heard only by island people. You saw it in their walk and in the performance of tasks.

"Don't hurt to ask around," he said.

"Is there anything you need or want us to find out?"

"I got what I need. Find out what you want to find out."

"You fished us right today," I told him.

"It's a big ocean, Mon."

We said we'd see him in the morning and I hauled on the stern line so Ciro and Michael could step up to the dock. The tide was really going out and the boat was sitting low. I climbed up last and waved goodnight to Ulis, but his head was down.

The bar was crowded. People in slacks, some in blazers and light jackets, stood in groups around the high chairs that were already filled. They all looked happy and well off and glad to see each other. Being in a boat all day made them that way and it wasn't bad listening to them carry on. The air conditioning was turned up, but it was warm near the people and in their good perfumes and aftershaves there was the smell of sun and the salt breeze of the afternoon.

Michael snaked his way to the bar for three scotches. He signed the room and carried them back to us. We touched glasses and Ciro made a face.

"It's like water. You wouldn't let them give your old dad a weak drink, would you?"

"Sorry, Pop. I'll get you another."

Ciro shook his head and worked his way to the bar. We saw him speak to the bartender who dumped his scotch and poured him a martini.

"Sneak," said Michael when he returned.

"Ought to be a silver bullet anyhow after that sailfish," Ciro said.

"Had him make it with gin, didn't you?"

"The very stuff."

I looked at Michael. "Bad?"

"The worst. Really affects him. He'll be miserable tomorrow. It's the juniper."

"I won't have many."

A committee woman began seating everyone. We walked by her and commandeered a table near the wall. The dining room filled up and Ciro asked if I saw anyone I knew.

"I think so."

A good-looking redhead in her early thirties walked in with another couple. She looked like a showgirl. Behind her, a handsome, dark man in very good shape, whom I knew to be at least fifty, followed. He'd inherited a surgical supply business at the age of twenty-eight, been married twice, once to an actress, and had built a marina in Charleston and one on the Ivory Coast.

"That's Jack Wells. I haven't seen him since I was a teenager. Real dollars there, men."

"Looks like young dollars," Ciro said, polishing off his martini and signaling for the waiter.

"His father made a fortune and I guess he didn't have any brothers and sisters to split it with. He had a 39 foot Rybovitch built when he was thirty-two, probably the youngest new boat owner they ever had. A few years back somebody told me he sold it and had a forty-four footer built. That might be the one we saw coming in this afternoon."

"Do you know him?" asked Michael.

"My father knew him. He might remember me. Maybe I'll walk over later."

Ciro ordered us three more and said, "That's some broad with him."

"He always had women, that guy."

Our drinks came and Michael watched the waiter set the clear one in the stemmed glass in front of Ciro. Ciro picked it up, looked at Michael and took a healthy sip.

"It's a good thing Mom isn't here."

"I was just having the same thought."

The dining room was filling up. Ciro selected a heavy burgundy from the wine list.

"It's a fish dinner, Pop. The fish or chicken bit."

"There ain't a decent white on that list. The wrong good wine will serve you better than the right lousy one."

"Well," I looked at Mike. "It's red snapper."

"Hat's off my sunburned head to you two men of the world." It was bright pink above his hairline. "Get it bad, did you?"

"On the way in, I guess. On the bridge with Ulis."

"Sneaks up on you," I said. "You don't feel it with the boat running in the wind. Wear a cap all day tomorrow."

When the salad came around, a couple in their sixties took two empty seats at our table and introduced themselves as Bill and Jane Clayton. Still a prospective buyer, Ciro asked what kind of boat they had.

"We sold our Matthews years ago. We're chartering for the tournament, a boat from the mainland."

"Those old Matthews' were great boats," I said. "My father had one before I was born. He always talked about it."

"We enjoyed that boat," Mrs. Clayton said. "It was a good boat for a lady."

Ciro said, "I wish my wife could hear you say that. We're half in the market now. As you can guess, I'm the half that's in."

Clayton said, "There's a Merritt in West Palm Beach I'd buy right now if I was still capable of doing everything myself."

"I'm new to all this," said Ciro. "I'm afraid I wouldn't know a Merritt."

"Wood boat," I told him. "Good fishing boat and comfortable. They build them up around Cape Canaveral."

"That's right," Clayton said. He looked at Ciro and nodded in my direction.

"This fellow your captain?"

"First Mate," Ciro replied. "He's my stockbroker, really."

"That so?"

"Quite right," I raised my glass. "And with a purpose. I'm down here trying to talk my client out of buying a boat."

"There's a strong case for that," Clayton said.

"I don't know," Mrs. Clayton said. "We really never regretted owning a boat. Although some years it seemed we couldn't afford it."

Clayton added, "And if you think you can't afford it, you're probably right."

"Whether I can or not depends on how well my stockbroker does for me."

"How has he done so far?"

"Not bad."

I had to grin. I'd done better than not bad and he knew it. I was still grinning when I looked out across the dining room and saw Mr. and Mrs. Hutchinson being seated with a stocky man who was probably in his late thirties, but who looked older. He was dressed in slacks and a Ralph Lauren Polo shirt like mine. Like me, he did not wear a jacket. My sister had been wrong or her information was old--they were together. I looked behind them, no longer grinning, feeling my chest break and looking toward the entrance to the dining room where a few waiters milled. Inez came in wearing a simple dark dress and carrying a handbag. Her hair was a way I'd seen before, back from her forehead, gathered and held in some way, and dropped just behind her shoulders.

I watched her walk to the table and join her parents and her husband, what had broken inside me running down the edges.

Clayton was speaking to me. I looked at him, probably looking like I felt.

"Did you hear what I said?"

"I'm sorry."

"I asked you what you thought of the market now."

"Oh. Well, it's a little harder this year. You need to be in the right names . . . " and I looked across the room again to The Hutchinson's table and Inez.

Ciro noticed. "Someone you know?"

I nodded.

"Go over."

"After they've finished dinner."

Clayton ordered wine for him and his wife. "Will you share a few of those names with me?"

I looked at the table a bit longer then I turned to him.

"I'll be happy to share them all if you'll open an account. My information's good and proprietary and my clients are like royalty to me. They give me their business and I try to do all I can. Can you see that it wouldn't be right to give those people's secrets away?"

"Put that way, I suppose I can."

"And I say it with respect."

"Thank you, Jim." Clayton looked at Ciro and nodded to him and it was like a salute.

Shrimp came around. I drank half a glass of wine and felt my stomach knot. It was like no time had passed at all. I hated the feeling and wanted it at the same time. I drained the rest of the wine in my glass and filled it and everyone else's.

Easy boy, I told myself. *Just easy.*

But I had to move or the knot in my stomach would pull open and everything would pour out for the world to see. It was a big dining room and there was no sign of the main course. People were table hopping.

"Excuse me," I set my napkin on the table. "I want to say hello to some people."

Clayton and Ciro said something, but I didn't hear it. My ears were burning from the wine but I wasn't drunk. Finding a path through the tables to the Hutchinson's I wished I was.

As I walked up I could see their faces. They were looking at me but I watched Inez. Her expression changed when she recognized me. She was the only one.

"Mr. and Mrs. Hutchinson," I held out my hand. "Jim Nielsen, do you remember me?"

Katherine Hutchinson gasped, "Why Jim, how are you? You've grown up. How long has it been?"

"A long time."

Hutchinson stood and shook hands.

"Yes," he said, "Yes, of course, Jim. It's good to see you."

I looked across the table at Inez, who watched nervously.

"Inez," I said, "you look wonderful."

She smiled then, manufactured a smile. She raised a hand. I reached across the table and took it. I didn't look in her eyes, not yet. I held her hand a moment then I let her go and turned to Barry who stood as Hutchinson had.

"Barry Rant," he said. "Nice to meet you." We shook hands and he put the pressure on like any dumb fraternity brother.

"We've met before. At The Cliffs a few years back." I turned to Inez. "Do you remember?"

"Yes," she said, nodding once.

"Sorry," he said, looking at me as if I were their waiter.

I could tell he'd had a lot to drink but he didn't look bad. Those guys never did.

Mrs. H. spoke up. "Sit down, Jim. How have you been and how is your mother?"

"I've been fine, thank you, and Mom is good. She's in Florida now."

"Sell that big old house you people had."

"Yes, ma'am."

"I loved that house."

"It got to be too much house for Mom."

Kate Hutchinson looked at her husband. They both looked very well, she a bit stouter.

"We'll have to visit her this winter."

"She'd like that. I don't get to see her much."

Mrs. H. nodded, smiling. It was time for someone else to ask something, to be polite at least. I almost turned to speak to Inez, but Hutchinson cut in.

"Are you down alone?"

"I'm down with friends. A client actually and his son."

"What kinds of clients do you have these days, Jim?"

"I'm a stockbroker."

"Ah," Hutchinson said, nodding. But he tightened a little. He'd probably been approached by more "friends" in the investment business than I could conceive. So I changed the subject.

"Did you folks do anything today?"

"Yes," Hutchinson said, finishing what remained in his glass. "We released two whites. Had fun with them."

"Great. Raise any blues?"

"No. No blue marlin yet."

Barry cut in like a knife. "Did you raise any blue marlin?"

"No. Released a nice sailfish is all."

There was still nothing from Inez, the only one I wanted to hear anything from. I looked at her then and into her eyes. There was no sweet eagerness, no light like I'd known. Practical. Apprehensive. Her eyes guarded something. It was disappointing. I gazed at a point on her forehead and asked her if she'd heard from my sister. She seemed a little relieved at the question.

"No. Not in some time. Ann and I have been lousy letter writers since we've been married."

She was handing it to me right off the bat about being married but I thought it was more to appease Barry. I glanced at him and he looked smug. In possession, the bastard. I thought about it a moment and decided I didn't give a damn.

"You look absolutely gorgeous, Inez. You really do." And, except for the eyes I no longer knew, she did.

"Oh," she said, as though amused. "Thank you."

No one said a word. I almost went further. For a moment I didn't care if I made trouble for her or not but then I didn't feel right about it so I turned to Mrs. H.

"And Mrs. Hutchinson you're as lovely as ever. You ladies are truly amazing."

I almost heard Inez sigh relief.

Mrs. H. beamed. "Aren't you the diplomat. If you think that crack will get you invited for a drink, you're right. Stop by the boat tomorrow afternoon."

"Thank you." I saw the waiters starting the main course around.

"I've got to get back to my table."

Hutchinson shook hands with me and Mrs. H. pecked my cheek.

Barry stood and we shook hands again.

"Good to see you," he said with great effort.

I reached across the table and took Inez's hand, but we didn't look at each other. There was no point in saying anything now.

I turned to her parents again.

"Good luck tomorrow."

"Good luck to you, Jim," said Mrs. H.

"Thanks for remembering us, boy," Hutchinson said. "Come by for a drink when it's over."

"That I will."

"And bring your friends."

"Thank you." I looked at Inez and nodded. Her head was down slightly but her eyes were on me. I said something else, about enjoying your dinner or something, but hardly heard myself speak. I slid through the waiters and around the tables to my chair.

Everyone was having a hell of a time. The red snapper was just arriving and Ciro ordered another bottle of burgundy. His eyes shined with the martinis and wine and no food yet. He held up his thumb and forefinger.

"This close," he told me. "I'm this close to buying that Merritt."

Everyone at the table looked stupid and a little drunk. I filled my glass and dug in to my snapper.

I swallowed and said, "That's great, so you're gonna buy a goddamn boat anyhow." It came out harder than it should have. Mrs. Clayton looked a little surprised.

"Yeah," Ciro said, as a matter of fact, I might."

"Well," I shrugged. "I'll have to work twice as hard to make you enough to pay for the damn thing."

Clayton got a laugh out of that and we all relaxed a little.

Ciro said, "That isn't all I had in mind."

"No?"

"Only partly. What I'll expect from you is some of that expertise I saw today."

"I get it," I said, calming down a bit. "You expect me to run the boat for you, too. The one I'll make it possible for you to own. You want me to be your captain."

"Captain wasn't exactly the title I was thinking of."

"That so?"

"Yeah. I was thinking more like deck hand."

"First Mate, huh?"

"In time, after you prove yourself. Second Mate to start. What do you say to that?" Ciro took a sip of wine and cracked a smile. Michael and Clayton chuckled softly.

I turned to Mrs. Clayton.

"Ma'am, kindly cover your ears."

We all burst out then and it was good. It cleaned me out and I drank some wine and finished dinner.

Clayton went into a tale of the first boat he ever purchased, an Egg Harbor skiff, which captivated Ciro. I looked across the room where The Hutchinson's ate slowly. I could move around in my chair and see them all. Barry was saying something to Mr. H., kissing his ass as he'd probably done from day one. Mrs. H. seemed to be listening as she methodically worked her knife and fork. Inez half listened, alternately looking at the table in front of her and down at her dinner. She poked what was on her plate over and over as though searching for one good morsel hidden among things she detested. She'd always eaten that way. She was the only person I knew who could find filet mignon or lobster in front of her and be melancholy about it. It was as if the process of eating itself was a little too harsh. You had to do it but you didn't have to like it. It only made her seem more graceful and I loved it like everything else about her.

I had to find a way to speak to her alone. I knew what she was feeling just then. I'll bet she wasn't ashamed to be married to him with anyone else but me.

Ciro was at me again, about the boat.

"Just look at it like a business. We'll charter her out. We wouldn't have to make it big, just pay her way. Is that done?"

"Uh-huh," I said. "It's done. But the expenses go up if you charter. Plus you need a rated captain with a ticket."

"What kind of ticket?"

Hundred ton, a hundred mile. That's what the insurance companies want. Good skippers don't come cheap."

Ciro sipped his wine and looked at Clayton, who nodded. "Your seagoing stockbroker speaks the truth."

"Yeah," said Ciro. "He usually knows what he's talking about. Before we hooked up, I was doing business all over the street. I had plenty of my own ideas about how to invest. He'd let me ramble on but in the end I'd always wind up doing what he said. Now I pretty much let him call the shots. He's got the best judgement I've ever seen in anyone."

I looked at Michael. "Am I actually hearing this?"

"He's drinking martinis. What do you expect?"

"Just don't get modest, Jim. And speaking of martinis, where's our waiter?"

"That'll be number four," Michael said. "It's liable to be a very complimentary night."

The waiter came around and Ciro placed his drink order, looking at his son.

"That's right, Mike. I'm in a complimentary mood. I was getting to you next, but now I think I'll go the long way around the table."

It was then that Inez placed her napkin on the table and stood. She took her bag and headed toward the hallway at the back wall where the restrooms were. I gave her a head start and excused myself. The lights started to go down, the tournament committee members were getting ready to speak. People who had been milling around returned to their tables and I walked around to the opposite side of the floor so no one would notice me. I turned up the far wall and entered the hallway and stood between the doors to the men's and ladies' rooms. People came and went each time either door opened. I tried to appear casual. She was in there a long time.

Then the door opened. She stepped out, looking down and saw me. She put her hand to her chest just below her neck very briefly and manufactured one of those smiles.

"You startled me."

"Let's talk, Inez."

"Come by the table."

"That's not what I mean."

She said nothing and the false smile faded. She knew exactly what I meant. She'd known since she'd first seen me and now it was coming. The tournament master was starting to speak.

"I want to talk to you alone, not here." I looked at her. The original beauty was still there, she would always have it. She had filled the slightest bit in places and it only added excitement to what had always been slender in design. I thought that her mother must have looked that way. She hadn't gotten much sun that day and her skin was creamy and unbelievably fresh-looking, but her eyes seemed strange, too bright. I thought I knew what it was.

"Meet me later on," I said.

"I can't."

"For Christ's sakes Inez, why not? Do you have any idea what it's like to see you again? You made me crazy for years."

"I didn't mean to."

"Of course not. And after that you kept me from going crazy." And quietly I added, "I love you for that."

"Don't say that."

"I've never stopped thinking about Block Island. Don't try to tell me you have."

"We were kids, Jim."

"Yeah. We were young. But it was love, Inez. It still is."

"You can't say things like that. I'm married."

"For a while you weren't."

"We're together now. He's been through a lot with me."

"You're drinking now, aren't you?"

"Not really."

"He's got you drinking like him. I can see it in your eyes. Come outside with me now."

"I can't. They're waiting for me."

"Tell them you don't feel well."

"No."

"You're making me crazy again. Come on."

She shook her head.

"What are you afraid of?"

"We shouldn't be talking like this."

"Oh, cut the shit."

"Don't swear at me."

"I'm not swearing at you. I'm in love with you. I've wanted to tell you that for years and now we're standing in this goddamn hallway. We had something and you know it. Won't you please give me a chance to speak to you?"

She looked at me and then out at the corridor. She could have walked right passed me, but she was standing there.

"All right," I said. "Later then. I'll come down by the boat."

"We have rooms."

"Meet me at the boat then. After midnight or whatever time you can get away."

She was still looking out the corridor. Then down at my feet. She shook her head.

"No, Jim." She kept looking down.

"Please, Inez."

"I can't." She moved lightly passed me. "I'm sorry."

I stood, not believing the last few minutes and how wrong they had gone. Then I began cursing myself. I went into the men's room and looked in the mirror. I hated the sight of my face. I stood with both fists clenched and ready to hit my reflection and send it in a hundred pieces, but the door opened and a man walked in. I pressed the faucet and threw some water on my face. My heart was drumming in my ears. I dried with a paper towel, wadded it, and slammed it in the bin and opened the door and walked out.

I started the long way again around the floor then turned and went for the door. An attendant opened it for me and I stopped, thinking I should at least say goodnight.

"Shit on it." I kept on walking.

Outside a group of Bahamians greeted me. One dressed in white, with a marina emblem on his shirt, asked me if I needed anything. I pressed a Bahamian bill in his hand.

"Get me a taxi, man."

He spun and shouted to four or five Bahamians who stood talking around an old white Chevy. They scattered except for one who dove behind the wheel. The motor turned over, the headlights went on and the Chevy pulled up next to me.

The guy I'd greased, opened the door for me and I slid in. The driver was a nervous, wiry black of about fifty, one of the few Bahamians I'd seen around who didn't wear a fishing cap of some kind. His hair was pretty gray and he turned around grinning and looked at me.

"Where you want to go, boss?"

"Town," I said. "Take me to town."

The car rumbled and shot forward.

"Here we go to town," he said. "But where?"

"Do you know what a shot and a beer joint is?"

"I think so."

"Good. Find one. The rankest, foulest, most fucked-up slop chute on this island."

"I know a place. She ain't no prize."

"Head for it."

"Not many white men go there."

"Floor it then."

"Get rough in there. Lotta fights."

"Right now I want to drink. If I fight later on I'll consider it a bonus."

"You in the mood tonight, boss. Something got you?"

"Yes, something's got me. What's your name?"

"Harold is my name."

"Harold, how much business do you do in a night with this car?"

"With the tournament on? Seventy-five, eighty U.S."

I took a hundred dollar traveler's check from my wallet.

"Here. No matter what shape I'm in, get me back by sunrise and I'll give you fifty more." Then I gave him my business card.

"What I do with this?"

"In case something happens to me or I wind up in jail. Call the number on that card."

He stuffed the check and the card in his shirt pocket and buttoned it.

"I'll keep you out of jail, Mon."

"Do what you can but don't worry about it. There's not much to worry about now."

We were bouncing down the sandy road farther than I'd ever been from the marina. I could see stars above the shapes of the sand pines. Then the trees broke and Harold swung the car onto the empty island highway. It was two-laned and paved, smooth as air after the jeep trail.

"Now we make knots, captain," he said.

The windows were halfway open and the moist rush of the cay filled the car. I remember thinking what a nice night it might be if I gave a damn about anything else. If my heart didn't pound like a jackhammer and my guts weren't in knots. I had known so many ways of being not alive and now this new way which was like falling through a storm. I set my teeth and clenched my fists. Harold slowed and rattled over a small bridge.

"How far is it?"

"A ways yet."

It was like I'd drunk nothing at all earlier. I was tight as a spring and my mouth was parched.

"Stop at the first place we can buy beer."

We passed some houses, shacks really, with and without electric lights. Then they were in clusters, dilapidated and too close to each other. They were like the little half-assed towns I'd seen in Asia that did nothing but depress me. Not the villages, the little farm, or fishing hamlets on the edge of some wilderness, them I always liked and the people in them. These were like the shanty towns slapped together, no one remembering how to farm or fish. The inhabitants worked in one type of rural industry or another. In some strange way they probably represented a better life, but were awful to see. It was better to pass them at night.

Harold slowed the car and pulled over at a tiny grocery of painted cinderblock. A few Bahamians of different ages stood outside in dirty T-shirts with bottles of beer. I went in and bought a six-pack of the coldest island beer I could find, got back in and passed one to Harold.

"Thanks, Captain."

I twisted the cap and emptied mine in two gulps. Then I took another from the cardboard, opened it and drank half in another long swig. It was like nothing.

"How far, Harold. I need something brown and heavy."

"We gaining on it."

"Put her in the corner then."

"She in there now."

We sped ahead a few more minutes then the car slowed and the road got bumpy and we were in town. There were a few locked up stores and a warehouse of some type, then an empty lot over-grown with weeds. Finally, I saw lights under a sign on the side of what looked like a barn that said Five Dogs.

There were a few beat up cars out front. We pulled over about twenty yards beyond it. There was no curb, just the line where the broken road ended and the dirt of the pathway began.

"Come on in with me," I said.

I got out and stood next to the car waiting for Harold. From the other direction I heard something cut the air. I turned in time to see a big, heavy Bahamian on a bicycle coming at me in the dark.

It looked as if he'd mow me down. I knew he wouldn't, he saw me and was just trying to have a little fun scaring me. He would veer off at the last second and miss me by inches. I was used to that shit in New York and usually ignored it but it wasn't the night for that. He flew by and I bumped a hard forearm against his. He grunted something and stopped and laid the bike on its side. He turned around and in an island accent called me motherfucker.

Harold was coming around the car. I told him to stay put and raised my hands.

"Let's go, man," I said.

He looked at me and moved forward. He was big and heavy and had a thick neck and arms. He wore a gray T-shirt and black shorts with high black sneakers and his head was shaved. He got about halfway to me then he turned and went back to the bike. I saw him fiddle with something around the handlebars and he came at me holding a chain.

"Fine," I said. "You need the chain, use it."

When he got within four feet I pivoted a quarter turn to the side and kicked him in the ribs and he stopped, still holding the chain. A group of Bahamians stood outside a boarded up building across the road. They came a little closer now that they had something to watch. When my dancing partner looked toward them I kicked him again in the same place. I felt the solidness of the strike in the heel of my moccasin and he dropped the chain in the dark alongside the car. Harold had come around behind me.

"What do you want me to do?" he asked.

"Nothing."

I didn't think he'd go for the chain now that he had an audience, but if he did I was ready to kick him in the face. I took a little chance, moving away from the car out into the street with my hands still up. I figured he knew the spectators, I was right, he followed me out in a half circle with a strange look on his face. I doubted he'd ever been challenged. He walked back and forth, not for any strategic reason, just to be doing something for the crowd. I stepped up and jabbed him twice with my left. I didn't get much, he was taller and I had to reach. He had his big hands and forearms up and he leaned back, away from the jabs.

His body was open between his elbows and I hit him a good right to his solar plexus. He didn't grunt or flinch, but his hands went down slightly and I hit him a left and right, a left and right and a couple of them were solid. He didn't like that and he covered his face so I buckled up and went to his body in flurries as if I were training on a heavy bag.

He stepped back and turned his back to me so I punched the back of his head. He didn't like that either, he turned and came at me like a bear. He was a lousy fighter, but very strong and he got me in an upside down choke hold. His fingers locked tight somewhere up around my ear and his forearm went up into my wind-pipe. I went down on my knees with his face pressing into my back, I reached up and worked on his fingers, but they were together like spliced rope and I couldn't breathe.

I uppercutted a right into his groin, but his arms restricted most of my stroke so it did me little good. I reached for a leg. I got both hands around his ankle and broke it loose, it took a long time, it was like trying to uproot a tree. He got even tighter around my neck as the leg went up and I was on the verge of blacking out, but I saw space under his foot. I choked, levering the leg high enough to get my shoulder under, raised up off my knees and his hold broke and he went over backwards like a felled tree.

I went down with him and we hit the dirt street side by side. I was faster getting up and wound up on top. He was on all fours and I rode him a moment, holding his shirt with my left and punching him in the back with my right. Then I felt hands on me, strong hands and four of them. They pulled at me and pulled me off.

"You'd better be a fucking cop," I hissed.

"I am a cop and you're under arrest, friend." The voice was calm and deep, but struggling with me.

I was wrenched free and tossed in the direction of Harold's cab. Hands had me again, against the grill of the cab with my hands spread on the hood. I turned and saw a lean, strong Bahamian in khakis and sneakers. Mine was the senior cop. The other had the bicycle man in the same position over the trunk.

The cop had me by the neck and the back waist seam of my trousers.

"Am I gonna have to handcuff you, mister?"

I couldn't answer him. I was completely out of breath.

"Eh, mister," he tightened his hold.

"No," I gasped. I was heaving like I hadn't taken a breath during the fight.

The cop eased a bit and said, "All right, I'm going to let you loose, but keep your hands on the car."

I nodded, still heaving. I was bent over the hood and I heard an old voice call my name. It was Sonny, standing out in front of Five Dogs with a plastic cup in his hand.

The cop asked me if I was down for the tournament. I nodded.

"You want to tell me how you got started on this?"

I was still catching my breath. "He cut me close on that bicycle and I shoved him out of the way."

Harold spoke up. "That one come at 'im with a chain, Mon." He bent and fished the chain from under the car where he'd kicked it and held it up for the officer to see.

I said, "He had it at the beginning, but he didn't use it."

My cop, asked for identification and asked if I thought I wanted to press charges. I shook my head. He walked around the car to speak to his partner. Sonny was standing next to me by then and I turned around and sat on the hood.

"Son of a bitch," Sonny said, grinning. "Somebody came inside and said there's a white guy beatin' hell outta Big Oliver. I couldn't see it was you until they pulled you off him. Then I figured I'd be bailing you out of jail tonight."

"You still might. It's early yet." I looked at my trousers. Both knees were ripped and caked with dirt.

Sonny stuck out his hand. "How the goddamn hell have you been all these years?"

I took his hand and squeezed. "All right, I guess." Then I winced.

"Hurt your hand on him?"

"Shoulder. Probably when I went down."

The cop walked back around to us and handed me my driver's license.

"Mr. Nielsen, it looks like either of you could have avoided this trouble. I'm sending you both on your way if you'll agree not to make no more work for us tonight. If you do I'll have to lock you up."

"Thank you," I said.

He put his pad in his pocket. "Enjoy your stay on Little Cay. She a peaceful place, we like to keep her that way. He nodded to his partner who motioned to the bicycle man who's face was beginning to swell. He picked up his bike, mounted it and looked at me contemptuously.

"Go on now," the other cop said.

Harold walked up and stood beside us. He asked if I was hurt.

"No." I looked at my elbow. It was raw and bleeding. "That's from the road. That and my knees."

Sonny looked at me in the streetlight.

"Your eye looks funny." He drained what was in his cup.

"That's from his arm. I don't think he landed a punch."

"You did though. I saw you."

I got one or two good ones in."

"One or two?" Harold spat. "If you hit him once you hit him ten times."

"Well," I said, watching the cops walk side by side down the street, "I swung at least that many."

Sonny said, "We'll get you a drink."

"We'll get me more than one. C'mon Harold."

We headed for Five Dogs.

"What are you doing down here?" asked Sonny.

"I'm here for the tournament."

"What boat are you on?"

"I'm not a deck hand anymore, Sonny, I'm a stockbroker. I chartered a Bahamian boat with some friends."

"Stockbroker, eh? You rich yet?"

"Not by anyone's measure, but I can buy tonight."

We walked in, the three of us, and stood at the bar. Sonny and I were the only white men in the place. Almost everyone had come outside for the tail end of the fight and I could feel them looking at me. I threw a U.S. twenty on the bar and held up three fingers.

Sonny set the plastic cup on the bar and said, "Another one of these."

I looked at the cup.

"Dark rum and tonic water," he said, "want one?"

I nodded and to Harold. "Make it three." I had caught my breath finally, but it burned when I breathed deep. At tables behind us things were being said about the fight.

I said to Sonny, "I yelled to you on the way out this morning."

He shook his head. "I never would have recognized you. You're as big as your father now that you're a man."

The bartender was as dark as Ulis with the same noble face. He set the drinks in front of us.

"Nice touch," I said, "these plastic cups."

"Unbreakable, Mon," replied the bartender. "We give 'em glass and they toss 'em at each other or me. Get tired a glass flyin' if you know what I mean."

"Cheers," I said, raising my cup.

Harold raised his. "To a good fighter."

"Who?" I asked.

"You, boss."

"That's right," Sonny said, tipping his cup.

"You're both full of shit."

Harold drained half his and set the clear plastic cup on the bar. He smacked his lips, the rum seemed to have an immediate effect on him, he looked at me and smiled.

"Where you learn to kick a man like that?"

"On board ship. A very wise man taught me it was hard to reach the groin because most street fighters instinctively protect it. But ribs are easy."

"You break his ribs?"

"I don't think so. At least I wasn't trying to. I just wanted him to drop the chain."

"You should break his ribs, he come at you with a chain that way," Harold said and took another drink.

I shook my head. "He had the chain because he was worried. He's probably used to pushing people around because he's so big, but he knew he was no fighter."

"You showed him he was no fighter," said Sonny.

"He just caught me on the wrong night."

Harold said, "I know you mad at somebody the minute you get in the cab, Mon. But who?"

"Only me, Harold."

He was about to say something, but before he could, a chubby, but strong-looking Bahamian in a dirty stripped shirt came up from one of the tables and shook my hand.

"You did good on Oliver. I never like that son of a bitch."

"Thanks, sir."

Two men from his table sat watching me. When I looked at them they raised their drinks. They were strong, hardworking men in their late thirties or forties and probably did everything simply and honestly and the best way they knew. The raised plastic cups looked ridiculously delicate in their rough, work-swollen hands and they grinned at me like friends. I wanted to buy them a drink, but thought it might insult them or the compliment they paid me. I raised my glass and nodded at them.

The guy who had come up nodded to Harold and Sonny and looked back at me.

"Good luck to you," he said, backing up.

"Thanks. I can use it. See you around."

Sonny watched me take a drink. I was calmed down and starting to cool off, but my breath was still sharp. I held the rum in my mouth a long time before I swallowed. It burned sweet all the way down.

Sonny squeezed my shoulder and ordered three more. "Goddamn, it's good to see you again. Have you been okay?"

"Sometimes I've been okay and sometimes I haven't."

He nodded slowly. "I was worried about you. We all were. We didn't know you were over there. When we found out we tried to get a mailing address, but nobody saw your mother."

"She moved. The mail was screwed up most of the time, anyhow."

"What was it like, Jim?"

I finished my rum and set it behind the new one.

"What I remember is not all bad, but being there was something else altogether. It was strange. After a while, I guess about halfway through it, I couldn't believe anything else had ever happened to me. And then I started to forget things."

"You lost your memory?"

"Only of things that happened before I went there. It was like I was cracking up yet I knew damn well I wasn't. I had a buddy named Andy. We got talking one time and he told me he was having the same thing. There was no history any more."

"How do you mean?"

I took a sip. "If somebody mentioned your name to me it would have taken me a while to remember who you were. It was like the old things had never been real."

"So you forgot about us."

"So much happened. I don't need to tell you. The first year back I would start sweating for no reason and my hands would shake. Not all the time, just once in a while. A long time after that I read somewhere that I wasn't the only one it was happening to. I read that what caused it was that the mind couldn't accept where the body was, couldn't accept it as reality. In other words, I couldn't believe I was actually home."

"Bother you now?"

"No. Not in years. There was nothing to do about it anyhow, no one to tell."

"Even the guys you were over there with?"

"None that came back live in my part of the country. Andy got killed. He was from Maryland. I wished he would have lived."

Sonny shook his head.

"One night some ARVN'S were catching it bad up in the hills. So off we went, a three-helicopter medivac with gunships for cover. They hit the lead bird just before it set down, really ate it up and we got hit a few times before the Cobras could work them over. We got everybody on board but Andy couldn't move. We held him on the floor next to the ARVN'S that were hit. I had to keep my headset on and could hear the pilots talking to the Med Crew back at the ship. Even if I could have taken the headset off you couldn't hear a damn thing over the turbines. The cabin was dark except for the instrument lights and all I saw was the outline of Andy's face. I didn't know he was dead until we landed. I never wrote his parents or went to see them after I got back. Nothing."

Sonny thought for a minute and shook a cigarette from his pack on the bar. He said, "You could have come around when you got back."

I looked at the rum in the glass. "I couldn't, Sonny. I couldn't bear to. Everything was gone."

"Not everything."

"Everything that mattered. When my father died my family lost quite a bit and I held on to Pete. And when that boat blew up, I knew my father was really gone. But that wasn't enough. I had to go ten thousand miles to watch more people die and not a goddamn thing came out of it."

"You came out of it, Jim."

"Yeah." I took a drink. "Big fucking deal."

"Don't talk shit."

Sonny signaled another round and I watched the bartender tip up the rum and the ice in the glasses turned brown. He topped them off with tonic water and set them in front of the three we were finishing. I looked across the floor where the guy in the stripped shirt sat with his friends. He nodded to me and raised a bottle of beer. I decided it was all right to buy them a round and motioned to the bartender.

Sonny said, "I know Pete was like a father to you."

"He had more patience than my father. We talked about everything."

"Your father was great, Jim. He was always swell to us and he didn't have to be."

"It was good that you guys liked him. You were rough char-acters to a young kid. You had all that salt and experience."

"Your old man had that. He was older than us and he had it in a more useful way. That's what we liked about him. He showed us how a man could be."

"Maybe he had too much of it. More than his heart could stand. Like too much of it kills you."

"Could be," said Sonny.

"Maybe it would have gotten Pete, too."

"Maybe, Jim. Either way, they both died too young."

I sipped my drink and asked, "Did you ever know anyone that knew as much as Pete?"

"He knew boats, that Pete."

"He knew boats and he taught me how to fish."

"Nobody could've taught you better."

I nodded, twirling my drink.

"He protected you from the rest of us."

I grinned.

"We needled the hell out of you because you were a nice kid. Pete wouldn't let us get too rough with you."

I thought of Pete then and of my father and suddenly I knew it was right that they wouldn't see me now.

"They both died knowing a bright-eyed kid."

"What?"

"Nothing," I said. And then, "I guess everything's different when you come back. I mean, what's different is you and you stay away from the stuff you used to know because it won't be the same. It meant a lot to you once and you don't want to risk it being any other way."

"Nothing much stays the same, Jim."

I nodded and drank.

He went on. "And that's not always bad. Look at you. You look like your father. You got his big shoulders and your mama's eyes. You made yourself something up there in New York. What's the matter with that?"

"I don't know."

"You done it all yourself. That big job you got and still enough in you to come down here and roll in the dirt with some island son of a bitch."

I shrugged.

"You see Jim. That's how your old man was."

"I guess so."

"Ain't no other way for a man to be."

I fiddled with my glass.

"I thought about Inez over there," I said, suddenly.

Sonny looked me over.

"Thinking about her kept me sane."

"Did it?"

"Yeah. Even though it was like she wasn't real, the thought of her kept me going. I told myself I'd try to find her, to see if she ever really happened."

"What do you mean?"

"I mean I wanted to see her again, is all."

"I figured you were sweet on her once but you ain't kids now. Also, she's married."

"I noticed. They were separated, weren't they?"

"Only for about six months. She came home to live and then she went back to him."

"He drinks, doesn't he?"

"No more'n me."

"He's too young to drink like you. And he's a sarcastic son of a bitch."

"What do you care, Jim?"

"What do you think?"

Sonny shook his head. "Careful, boy. She's married and a little tied up."

"That's not what you wanted to say."

"That right? What do I want to say?"

"You wanted to tell me that it wouldn't be any easier if she was single."

Sonny shrugged.

"What the fuck does his family do?"

"They do a lot. They lease some buildings from Hutch."

"Is that how Inez met him? How romantic."

"The families have known each other a long time."

"Sure," I said. "Their ancestors got rich together."

"Why are you getting into all this?"

"Because that son of a bitch doesn't love her and she can't love him."

Sonny made a face.

"Are you going to tell me that she does?"

"I'll tell you this, it ain't for you to know about."

"Why do you say that, Sonny? A few minutes ago you were telling me how swell I am with my shoulders and shit."

"And I meant it."

"As long as I don't go after Inez. Isn't that what you mean?"

Sonny pushed his glass forward. "It's two good families and they're married and you need to respect that."

"He's a slob. Why do you defend him?"

"I don't. He's her husband. He's Hutch's son-in-law."

"Yeah, well I want her."

"What right you got to her?"

"This, I've loved her since I was a kid."

"Well she didn't marry you, did she?"

"I wasn't around. Besides, I didn't have any kind of career then and I hadn't learned what going off someplace and being close to dying meant."

He picked up his drink as if he didn't hear me.

"Yeah," I went on, "I was real scared over there and half crazy, but I couldn't forget her. Now I'm five years back and I still can't."

"Well you better," Sonny said.

"Don't you tell me what I can and can't do, you goddamn Rybovitch captain."

I shouldn't have called him that. It was an expression they had used around the docks for lazy, drunken captains that no one else could afford to keep.

"Christ," said Sonny. "I ain't heard that one in years."

"I didn't mean it."

He shrugged. "You're not the first one to call me that. Besides, you're right."

Harold had been quiet a long time. He'd turned his stool the other way a bit so as not to listen, but now he looked at both of us. My voice had been loud enough for the guy with the striped shirt to hear and he looked at me as well with a nervous expression."

"Jesus," I said to Sonny quietly. "Can't you see what she means to me? I'm not trying to cause trouble."

"Then stay away from her."

I shook my head. "Not until I know she doesn't want me."

He sighed and pulled a cigarette from his pack.

"It was different when you were kids. She ain't like that anymore."

"She could be. She needs to be, in fact. Being married to him hasn't done her any good. She's drinking now, isn't she?"

"Some."

I nodded. "I can see it in her eyes. He's got her drinking."

"The two of 'em ain't that bad together."

"Don't say that to me, Sonny. You've known her since she was a baby. You think I didn't notice how you treated her like a queen, how safe you always kept her around that goddamn boat? You loved the same thing in her that I did."

"She grew up, got married and complicated. Don't expect her to be any other way than she is."

"I ain't about to give up."

"Do what the hell you want, then." He stood and picked up change from the bar. "I got to get back. We're sailing tomorrow."

I'd forgotten about the tournament. I asked Harold the time.

"Eleven-thirty, boss." He'd been belting them back out of the cash pile in front of me and Sonny.

"You okay to drive?"

"Not bad to drive."

"Come on," I said to Sonny. "We'll run you back."

That we left together and friendly relaxed the guy in the striped shirt and his friends. I waved to them on the way out and they nodded to me in a way that said I would always be welcome there or in any other place in which they would be.

It was good to be outside, out of the smokey bar. We walked to the car and I stopped Harold from getting in behind the wheel. "You navigate," I told him. "I'll take the helm. I've been drinking all night, but I'm cold sober."

"You sure, Mon?"

"I couldn't get drunk tonight if my life depended on it."

"Okay, but be easy with her when the road is rough. She's a little tired."

"Smooth as glass, Harold."

Sonny got in back and I headed off slowly through the un-paved part of town that was mostly dark. The car was old, but ran well and was solid, I could tell Harold babied it. It was tough to keep a car running well off the mainland. Our beams found flying insects, small rodents crossing in the dust, and every so often, groups of three or four men walking in the dark. Every one of them stopped to look at us, not to identify us, but to verify something. Faces dark in the headlights, staring as we drove up, never waving, I felt them watch us a long time after we passed.

Sonny and I didn't speak. I followed the glow of his cigarette in the rearview mirror as it came to his face and burned bright. Harold sung softly, alternately giving me directions and picking the rhythm back up.

"Down in de market you can hear,
Big lady shout,
Aqui is rice, Salt fish is nice,
But rum is fine any time of the year."
He pointed. "Turn here, Mon. This road."

I slowed and the lights fell on a small sign for the marina. I turned in and we were back in that palm and sand pine thicket, a shade darker than the night. It was the same dirt road and I crawled the car. The moon had risen above the cay, not quite full quarter, like a swordfish tail.

"Don't be sore at me," I finally said to Sonny.

"I ain't sore."

The road curved around to the marina lights and we passed the generator shed and came to the line of boats in front of the marina. Some of the cabins of the boats were still lit, but the dock was quiet. I thought I would walk the docks all night until I was tired enough to sleep. I stopped the car near *The Katherine*.

"You got me back before morning, Harold. Dented, but out of jail." I got out and took fifty U.S. from my wallet.

"Thanks, Boss. I wish you luck in the tournament and in all other things."

"Luck to you, Harold. Can you drive all right?"

"Sure." He put the car in gear.

"You still a good fighter," he said and the car moved away from us.

I walked Sonny to the boat. He pulled a stern line and hopped aboard and turned and looked at me.

"Leave it alone, Jim. It's no good for you, either."

"You don't know everything," I said.

I turned and started up the dock. There was a little wind from the southeast and the heat from the afternoon was gone. I felt the breeze on the back of my neck and saw a woman walk up and stand just out of beams of the docklights ahead. It was Inez.

She looked at me and then down at the boat. Sonny saw her and muttered something and opened the wheelhouse door. He slid it shut behind him and when the light went on inside I walked to her. She had put a sweater on over her dress.

"What were you going to do if I didn't come?"

I shook my head. "Follow you home, I guess. I don't really know. But here you are."

"I'm here because I know you'd keep trying to see me. And because I don't want you upset anymore than you've already made yourself."

"Are you going to tell me that you're happy, Inez?"

"Are you going to tell me that you are?"

"Of course not."

She looked down at my chest and said, "Maybe some people can be happy. Maybe other people just stop thinking about it. They slip into a life and know it's the only one they can live."

"Come on," I said. "Let's walk."

I touched her arm and we walked together out of the docklight, down the line of silent yachts stretched tight against their lines in the current, beyond the last row of pilings to the gravel drive, across it and to the trail that led through the coconut groves and sand pines to the ocean.

We said nothing and made no sound walking on the sand of the trail. Light from stars through breaks in the fronds overhead fell to the floor of the grove like a broken mosaic. Once, walking, when that light fell on Inez and when her shoulders and folded arms and hair were the light from those stars I whispered something and heard her sigh.

We walked and, in through the pines, the air was sweeter and like the ocean and then we saw the glow of the beach and the sea.

Not looking at each other, we slipped off our sandles and loafers and I followed her. She walked with a sandle dangling from each hand, sometimes looking down and her hair would hang to the sides of her face and then looking up again letting her hair back. I walked behind her, loving her hair and the way she stepped along.

We walked to the ocean. There was no sea, we were on the leeward side of the cay and tiny swells broke on the sand like lake waves. Up the beach a cypress log had blown up in a storm and the sand had piled around it from other storms. I took Inez's arm and walked her to it and we sat on the trunk that was flattened from the natural growth of the tree and smooth from the wind and we sat moving our feet in the sand and looked at each other.

I thought then of the first summers on the dock when I didn't know yet that I loved her. She looked at the sea and so did I, like two people who knew the sea well and loved it anyway. It was very dark, but we could see far out in it, it was moving, and then above it where the sky started, light with stars. There were so many stars. A broken shell of moon hung low.

I said, "I like it when the moon's little like that."

She looked at me. "Why?"

"A big moon's too bright. It steals the secrets from the night."

"Do you have secrets?"

"I used to. Up on the carrier deck when I looked at the sea at night or at the sky. And down below when I slept in the dark. You were my secret."

It was like speaking for the first time. As though the talking I had done all night, the trip down, the last five years of my life meant nothing. I went on, listening to my voice.

"I used to think of the hurricane. I used to save it to think of."

"So did I," she said.

"You didn't say two words to me on the trip home. You wouldn't even come up on the bridge when I spelled Sonny."

"I thought we'd done something terrible."

"We did. We wasted perfectly good opportunities to make love again."

"I was a virgin. Can you believe that?"

"I never once thought about it. But I guess that's an accomplishment for anyone that roomed with my sister for a year."

She grinned. "You were only seventeen, weren't you?"

"All of sixteen and also a cherry."

"Dear me, I ruined you."

"Nineteen year old virgins haven't ruined many men."

"We were just kids. God, it was wonderful."

"Of course it was, didn't you know it then?"

"No. Not for a long time. I just know that you were Ann's brother and much younger. I just felt guilty about it."

I was quiet a long time. Then I looked at my feet and spoke to her.

"You were ashamed, too, weren't you, Inez? That I was a deck hand and not rich."

"No."

"Please don't lie. If I would have been one of those charming little in-breds from the Yacht and Tennis Club you would have felt different about it."

"Not if they were only sixteen. Not if they were my roommate's brother."

"You don't give a damn about that. I was that nice kid on the dock whose father died and lost the family business and had to sell their boat and hung around doing odd jobs and mating on the only charter boat in that seagoing prep school of a yacht basin."

"Don't say that."

"I know how some of those private boat owners used to look at me. Like I was a stray dog."

Inez's eyes grew round and blinked.

"Just as long as you ignored me from that point on you were safe, right, no matter what I said to anyone. Even to Ann because you ignored her, too."

She looked down and her hair hang over the sides of her face again and her head shook a few times. I dug a handkerchief from my back pocket and pressed it in her hands.

"Well, I never told her, Inez."

"I'm so ashamed."

"I never told anyone except someone you don't know named Andy and he's dead now. He wasn't in any yacht club either."

"God, I'm so sorry, I was just afraid and I didn't know anything. I thought no one would understand if they found out."

"What difference would it have made if anyone understood or not?"

"Don't be ridiculous. We were just kids. Would you like to have explained everything to my father?"

"I would have gladly explained to him that I loved his daughter."

"I don't think he would have been so reassured to hear something like that from a sixteen year old."

"Then I'll explain it to him now, as a twenty-seven year old."

"You can't feel that way about me, Jim."

"I can and I do."

"Well you shouldn't. I'm married."

"For a while you weren't."

"I went back to him. It was my fault anyway."

"I don't believe you."

"It's the truth. It was because of me."

I shook my head.

"I was miserable. Nothing was ever perfect enough for me, I complained about everything. Barry couldn't live with me like that, so I left."

"Maybe it was your husband that wasn't perfect enough for you."

"No. I went into therapy and it helped. I'd been depressed for years."

"Over what?"

She looked at the night ocean as though it were her troubles.

"Things," she said, looking out. "Things about being a little girl. Things about my mother dying and leaving me alone."

"I know those things, Inez. I knew that you felt them. You were a lonely girl and hurt and beautiful and I loved you for it the same as I love you now."

"No, Jim," she said, quietly and her hand held my forearm.

"Why the hell not, Inez? What do you see beyond his wealthy family? What made you marry him?"

"He was there for me and seemed right. I found him attractive."

"Yes, he's very attractive. Did you find him in a beauty contest?"

"Are you going to be like that?"

"I'm sorry. But, aside from his monied background, I just don't see the pull."

She held my forearm a bit firmer to quiet me. We sat for a moment and her palm slid past my wrist to my hand and she held it in both her hands.

"We've been married six years, Jim. We weren't apart that long. Barry wanted me back as soon as I had gone. We met and talked about it and then he started to court me again and I knew how much he needed me. I have to be needed, Jim. That's important to me. Most of the time our life is good and it's a busy life. We travel and we do quite a bit socially. We like to entertain."

"Is entertain a euphemism for drink?"

"Everyone drinks, Jim."

"Barry certainly does, not that I care. But I'm told you do, too."

"By, whom?"

"It doesn't matter. I can see it in you. And you're only thirty."

"We drink and our friends drink. I don't drink any more than anyone else."

"You wouldn't need to drink if you were with me. You wouldn't need as much crap in your life. Don't tell me Barry's been the faithful husband, either."

"I won't. We've had our problems with that."

"Jesus, how could any man cheat on you?"

"They could if I made them miserable enough."

"He'll never love you the way I do. He won't take as good care of you."

"I know you, Jim. You've a way to go and you're going to get there. You wouldn't be able to put up with someone like me on the way."

"Are you kidding? All I want to do is take care of you."

"You say that now, and you might feel that way now, but you won't later. You'll resent me for being such a cry baby and for taking so much of you."

"I want you with me."

"I'd only hold you back."

I looked offshore at the darkness where the ocean lay moving, knowing. I looked a long time.

I said, "I would think of you on nights like this and one time you saved me."

"I did?"

"Yes."

"How?"

"You shouldn't know. But I'll tell you this, in a real bad time, weeks of it and things only getting worse, I started to look at our wake behind the ship like it was a friend, like stepping off would have been the kindest thing I could do for myself. I was so broken, Inez, so worn down and there was nobody. My friend was dead.

"One night I looked behind the ship a long time and probably would have done it, but I was so tired that I crawled out on a catwalk and lay on my side, listening to the water pass by below me. I fell asleep and dreamed I was young again and of you in the lighthouse—I had forgotten about it and when I woke, the sun was up and it was a beautiful day and I thought that the same life I was in, bringing what was in that dream had brought me you and I was all right because I knew then that I had to live, if only to prove you were real. You kept me from falling apart."

"I should have written you."

"I wished for a letter, but never expected one."

"If I'd only known, Jim."

"It's all right. I could think of you when I needed to and when I saw something beautiful."

"Was anything beautiful?"

"Yes. The country was beautiful. The hills were high and bright after the rains and the light was beautiful. There's no light like the Asian light."

"Were you frightened?"

"On and off. The fear is mostly when you're new. After a while you stop caring what happens to you and you reach a point where you miss being frightened. It just all goes grim as though nothing else ever happened before or you resent what you did because it was too good in comparison."

"Did you ever hate me, Jim?

"Nothing could make me hate you. I hated my luck, though, and I guess I hate your husband. I hate that he doesn't deserve to have you."

"Did you look for me when we separated?"

"I couldn't. I was hungry and groping and trying to make it as a broker. I had no right to look for you. I was too poor."

"Your family wasn't poor."

"We weren't wealthy. Not really."

Inez looked at me and really smiled for the first time.

"You were very responsible as a teenager. It was so safe if you were there. When Ann and I used to let you tag along it was to protect us."

"I think I knew that."

"And on Block Island, in that storm." She sat close, looking at me.

"You believed in me on that trip."

"Yes. In a serious, gangling sixteen year old."

"How do I seem to you now?"

"Changed. Tight in the face. Still a boy's face but solemn. Your eyes are older but they still shine. God, how your eyes always shined."

"It was your eyes, Inez, that haunted me for years. There was a secret in those eyes only I knew. I never loved anyone else."

"I loved you in that storm, Jim."

"Love me now."

"We can't love now."

"You could come to New York when you could. We could love that way."

"People like us don't love like that."

"Then I'm asking you to leave him."

She shook her head. "It's working now. We've decided to have a baby."

"Are you pregnant?"

"I don't think so. Not yet."

I kicked at the sand with my heel.

"But it was real between us, Inez. I mean, it was you, wasn't it, with me in the lighthouse that day?"

"It was the best love I've ever made. You were so sweet and a man for so young. I was afraid that no one would ever care that much about me again."

"Did anyone ever?"

"I don't think anyone else could."

"Isn't that reason enough?"

"To disrupt my life again? Would you want me to do that?"

"If you were unhappy, I would."

"But I'm not unhappy, Jim. I may not be happy every moment, but I can live the life I'm living."

"It just doesn't sound like that much."

"To me it is, Jim."

I shook my head and kicked the sand.

She said, "Will you try and understand?"

Slowly, I buried my feet to the ankles and pulled them loose and smoothed the sand over with my toes.

I said, "I don't know which will be the least bearable, thinking about you or not being able to think about you."

"No one says we have to forget each other. It doesn't have to be that way."

"Are we supposed to send Christmas cards?"

"What would be so bad about that?"

"Aside from tearing my insides out, probably nothing."

She was close and she held my arm and pressed against it.

"Be my brother," she said,

"What?"

"I always wanted a brother. Will you be that?"

"I'll have to think that one over."

Something came off the land behind us, not cool and not a real wind, but I knew it was there. I slipped my arm loose and around Inez and held her to me.

"Big brother or little brother?"

"Both."

"Does being a brother mean I can't kiss you? Even tonight?"

"Well, just tonight, Jim. Just this once."

I brought her close for a long kiss and it was the way I had remembered it.

"I'll be your brother, Inez, and if you ever leave him, I'll be something else."

"Don't waste any of your life waiting for that."

"It's my life to waste."

"Don't say that."

"You don't know."

"Yes I do."

"You do?"

"Yes."

"Come here."

I kissed her and we looked at each other and thought of the island in the storm and we started to kiss again as boy and girl, knowing there was nothing beyond the kissing and I felt Inez believing in me again, as strong as the wind against the lighthouse had been.

We stayed there a long time. We kissed and held each other and Inez nestled in my neck and fell asleep and I whispered to her as she slept against me. The little waves were quiet on the beach and the night was quiet and I watched the paths of stars and the moon go down.

Before the light came I woke Inez and we walked the beach beneath the untroubled sky to the sand road. I walked slowly, still holding her, through the vague, astral light of the palm grove.

The dock lights were still on. Sonny was up and watched us coming. I kissed Inez on the cheek and she started sleepily toward the cluster of rooms at the private end of the marina.

"Did you get any sleep at all," I asked Sonny.

"No," he said.

"Is there anything you want to say?"

"I ain't the one with something to tell."

"That so? Then listen to me and listen good. Nothing happened with me and Inez since you saw us last. We did some talking, is all."

"The two of you must have had quite a conversation."

"Look, I don't care what you think about me, but you better not think anything about her."

"All right."

"And I won't have anyone else think it, either."

"All right, all right. I was the only one on the dock when the two of you came walking up, anyway."

"Do you believe me, Sonny?"

"Yeah, I believe you."

"Then shake my goddamn hand."

And he did.

I walked down the dock to *The Tina* and hopped aboard. The lights were on below. Ulis stood in the galley, drinking a cup of tea in his underwear. He watched me come below and strip and throw my clothes on my bunk. I put on a swimsuit, took a bar of soap in its plastic container, toothbrush, and toothpaste, and a towel and climbed back up to the cockpit. I turned on the dockside water and wet myself with the hose and lathered my hair and face and body. The soap stung my elbows and knees and they started to bleed a little. I rinsed and toweled myself and brushed my teeth and spat over the side. I passed Ulis for the third time on my way below. He looked at me, still drinking his tea.

"What happened to you?" he asked.

I was pulling on a pair of clean shorts.

"Just about everything."

CHAPTER VII

When Ciro and Michael came down the dock, the sun was molten pink and climbing over the line of palms on the beach that ran to the inlet. It was a clear morning and light blue and the sea beyond the jetty was smooth and darker blue and rippled with the breeze that was coming with the sun.

A few boats were idling out in a line and I watched them reach the inlet and add power, one after the other. They rose and dipped through the jetty and beyond it and ran out into the first soft sunlight. The weather was right, very right, and my blood started like a tidal rip. I filed hooks, wound new leaders, and squared away gear like a madman.

"What the hell are you doing?" Ciro asked me, walking up.

"Getting ready to win this tournament."

Michael handed me a container of coffee. "We figured you scored last night."

"Not exactly."

He looked me over and then out toward the inlet.

"Looks like another calm day."

"Perfect," I said.

Ulis started both engines and I hopped out on the bow and cast us off and felt the hum of the engines through the deck like a life. I moved back along the side of the wheelhouse and jumped back down into the cockpit where Ciro and Michael had the stern lines loose and were throwing them on up like two pros. The boat moved forward, clear of the slip, and Ulis turned us. Ciro, Michael, and I stood together watching the dock and the other boats getting ready to go out. We moved passed each one, their bows slid toward us and fell back, nearly all the boats were painted white, the engines running in some, and people walked up and down the dock with last minute stuff and I looked at the orange rising light in the clubhouse windows and the white mast of the flagpole with the tournament flag and the flag of The Bahamas flying above it.

I slapped them both on the back.

"What?" Michael turned to hear me above the engines.

I grinned and pried the lid from the coffee container I'd left on the cooler.

"What happened to your knees?" asked Ciro.

"Skinned 'em." I took a sip.

Ciro looked at me. "He got your neck, too."

"Not much of it."

"I don't suppose you got any loran numbers or anything like that out of the deal?"

"Nothing we don't already have."

"The night was a total loss then?"

"I haven't decided yet."

He looked at me owlishly. I rubbed the top of Michael's head with my fist.

"Now what?" he said.

"This is the day," I told him.

"Think so?"

"I'm sure of it."

I drank the coffee and took the rods from their racks in the wheelhouse and set them butt first in the holders in the cockpit. I picked two rigged ballyhoo and two rigged mullet from the cooler and set them aside from the other baits.

When we passed *The Katherine* only Sonny was on board. He was busy in the cockpit and couldn't see me, but I waved anyhow and Ulis added throttle and we followed a big Pacemaker through the inlet. On both sides of the jetty, kids stood on the rocks waving. The red release pennant was still up from the sailfish and the older kids knew what that meant and they liked that Ulis was our skipper, they waved to him, really, island-born and a natural fisherman like them.

I climbed the ladder to the bridge. The Pacemaker cleared the rocks and turned northwest. The other boats outside had already headed that way. I saw them strung out all the way to the horizon. Ulis pushed the throttles up to cruise and steered south. He looked at me and I nodded.

We ran thirty minutes. To our starboard, Andro's coast rose up flat and covered with sand pine that seemed blue in the new light. The day before on the same course we hadn't seen the beach, but now it was so clear that individual treetops appeared plainly and we saw the rest of the island that ran southeast.

Bonito broke the surface, they weren't much bigger than baitfish, they flew in an arc like little footballs and birds circled over them in frustration. They were too large to swallow, but the birds stayed with them, hoping they'd lead them to bait.

We passed the birds on the same heading. The sun was higher, harsher already and all of the sea to the southeast was like silver fire to the edge of the world. I watched it as we ran, as though that part of sea and everything south of it was ours to keep for as long as the sun held. We glided south. On the bridge there was no noise from the engines and no vibration, only the vee of the hull furling seas that welled up and out in flat, clear sheets and fell beside the boat with a sound like water from a falls. We planed that ocean like a giant sea bird.

Ulis didn't speak. I knew there was no place in particular he wanted, no point off Andros, no precise depth. He was waiting for a stretch that felt right. When he found it, the water unbelievably dark and clear and more fathoms deep than I could conceive, he brought both throttles slowly back and the water stopped crashing around us and we pitched gently and rolled, more like the ocean than a creature flying over it.

I climbed over the side of the bridge and let both outriggers down. Then I lowered the release flag, unwound the leaders on two baits, dropped them over and let them back and ran the lines up the halyards. Ulis watched them skip and slowed the boat a touch.

I staggered the flat lines closer in, they rode a little smoother in the calm behind the stern. Then I took the biggest rigged squid from the cooler, a real monster a foot and a half long and put him on the fifth rod which I handed up to Ulis. He freespooled the reel and the squid fell back. Ulis stopped the reel with his thumb and the squid made a wake dead center behind the other baits. He dropped it back thirty more feet until I had to look a long time to find it from the cockpit.

Michael watched it, too.

"What science fiction movie you get that thing out of?"

"The one where the bait eats the crew."

"That's a horse of a squid, all right," said Ciro.

I watched it trail us like a dingy. "I just hope some barracuda doesn't get brave and ruin it."

It looks too big for one to mess with," said Michael.

"You'd be surprised what something'll try when it gets hungry enough," I said.

Ulis kept us headed south, in deeper water and the big island fell farther to starboard until the low shine of the beach was difficult to see. Nothing hit. And I wasn't seeing anything, but I liked the way the baits trolled and I felt the day was right. It was a feeling I had every so often when Pete was alive.

I watched our wake while the morning sun started to burn my face and neck. A few light clouds made up over Andros. Though I hadn't slept, my head was clear and my eyesight exceptionally sharp. My neck was raw from the fight, my right shoulder was sore and my elbow and both knees were bruised, but it only made me feel more alive. It was the first time in a long while that I wasn't angry or longing for something. I wanted to fish and nothing else. I stayed on the gunwale about an hour, checked the baits and climbed up on the bridge with Ulis.

Around ten, the sun was very high to our starboard and the water was the deepest blue I had ever seen. A long brown weedline stretched ahead of us like an island. It was three times wide as the boat and I couldn't see the end of it. There was bound to be bait under it. Ulis turned the boat to starboard to skirt the side.

I shook my head.

"We'll cast a shadow. Work the other side."

He looked over his shoulder at the sun, understood in a second and swung the wheel.

I looked all the way around us. There were no other boats in sight.

I said, "Let's take our time and work all of it. We got it to ourselves."

I looked for shadows under the grass or something running unlike the current. There were a few pieces of drift in the grass, palm fronds, planks, and on one a bird sat waiting. He turned to watch us roll by then he stretched his wings, flapped up and passed us. I watched him. He banked and spun down with a splash and got something. We trolled by him again and half a baitfish hung from his mouth. He stretched his wings, protective of the catch and jerked his neck straight to swallow. I watched him until Ulis punched my arm and pointed.

Out from our side of the weedline two black natural shapes protruded several inches from the surface. They were like dark tops of halfmoons and at least six feet apart.

My heart drummed in my chest.

"Work him gentle," I said. "He may be asleep."

"We should have a teaser out."

"If he don't spook I'll rig one for another pass."

"Might not get another pass."

"I know, Ulis. Don't crowd him."

Ulis eased the bow to port a bit.

"Right like that," I said. "He'll either like 'em or he won't."

We saw him turn and lie still in the water, cooly and angrily.

Ulis said, "He got the scent."

I was afraid to say anything, anything at all. But I knew it wasn't scent, not yet, only impulse, natural urge. We passed where the big fish had worked the edge of the weedline thirty yards to our right, so slowly and efficiently he appeared to be part of it. He'd stalked the edge, using the current and the angle of darkness under the woven mat of weeds as quietly and as careful with his shadow as we had been. I thought of him in those shadows, huge angry eyes searching for something to rush and strike.

And now there was another thing, something on his other side that he didn't know about. It made a vibration plowing along, a flash of bronze propeller and sea rushing off its strakes like a small storm of crushing water, a steady sensory signal like a churning school of frightened bait. It quickened the marlin's heart and he turned to swim in slashing. To kill two, three, five with each rush, dive like a rocket and swallow them all whole and in one pass as they sank crippled and dying then turn again and start up madly into the school for another slashing run.

He could take fifteen or twenty small fish that way, but he was curious about what moved the school and the mating prospects thereof. The bigger bait would be scattered along the trailing edge of the school anyhow and he was unconcerned about other mature males that had lay claim to females or the school because he was a big marlin and had not run from anything in a long time.

We watched the baits, the four little wakes of mullet and the lone wake of the big squid farther back. I wished I'd had time to check each bait. We had come up on the weedline so fast.

I stood facing astern, both hands on the stainless steel rail that went around the bridge. I was ready to slip through and ease myself down to the cockpit.

The baits were about even with where the fish had been. I looked for him but couldn't even see a swirl where he'd gone down. Then there was a smooth bulge of water and a powerful flash of green and blue behind the starboard outrigger. Water exploded at the bait and the pin popped and he was gone.

"Jesus," I said, never seeing it happen so fast. I saw the flash of green again, twenty feet ahead of the water he'd broken.

"He's after the flat line," Ulis said from behind me, but I was already slipping through the rail, easing myself down like the end of a chin up, careful to land lightly. A loud bump could ruin it.

I came down next to Michael. I pushed him into the fighting chair and was at the flat line just as the fish hit it. I flipped it to free spool, but there was nothing.

I cursed.

Ulis shouted, pointing to the other corner of the stern.

I darted across the deck to the other flat line and this time I had the rod in my hands and was passing it to Michael when I saw the fish come up, water flying. The clothespin popped and I felt him a second, but before I could freespool the reel he was gone.

"C'mon," I said. "C'mon." I looked at the port outrigger, knowing something was wrong. It had the biggest mullet and he was close to it, but the halyard never moved and the clip was quiet.

Then it hit me like a brick.

"SPEED THE BOAT!" I screamed. "THAT'S WHY WERE LOSING HIM."

Ulis spun and touched the throttles and the sound of the motors changed. I yanked the rod from Michael's chair, shoved it back in the rod holder and raced across the deck to my old place on the gunwale and hopped up. I strained to look at the water behind the outrigger and, without turning around, asked Ulis if he saw him.

"No," said Ulis from above. But he wasn't turning the boat around yet. Ciro had come out to the cockpit and stood behind the chair. He was turning to look up at me when I heard Ulis again.

"There he is, Mon."

All the way back, fifty yards behind us, the marlin came slow and deliberate, not a sideways wild rush like the outrigger and flat lines, but a smooth, swimming strike from behind. He followed the last wake, the biggest one we made. I saw his bill first, inches out of the water, tense and scissoring, methodically killing.

"He's after the squid," I said, hopping down and turned in time to see Ulis take the rod from the holder. Then Ulis and the rod did something like the first frantic dance of a water searcher with a willow limb. He struggled with the rod a moment and flipped the reel on free spool.

I held up my hands. Ulis passed the rod over the rail and down to me and I held it, my thumb on the spool, watching the line reel with my thumb already burning up. I walked the rod to Michael in the chair, got the butt in the gimbal and his hands on the rod.

"What do I do?" he asked, quickly.

I still had my thumb on that spinning spool.

"Hold him just like that. He's swimming away with the bait."

I looked up at Ulis who stared behind the boat. After a few more agonizing seconds, he looked at me and nodded.

"Put it to him," Ulis said.

"Hold tight that rod, Mike," I said and reached across him and flipped on the drag.

Then the rod went down like a sapling and the reel was singing and paying out line slower, but just as steady.

"Haul back that rod," I said. "Right up to your chest."

He yanked the rod back and everything tightened in his arms. Then he eased and the rod went forward and down and I told him to do it again.

"Whoa." Michael said, feeling that incredible animal power. It was his first real fish and I knew he was a little afraid.

"Good," I said as calmly as I could. "He's got a hard, boney mouth. Use your back and legs and set that hook one more time and deep."

"Okay," he said and grimaced. He arched backward, not used to the maneuver, but understanding what it was supposed to do. He arched and curled the rod with all he had, but it stopped six inches short of his chest.

"My God," he said, forcing a grin and easing the rod forward. The line was really going out now. The fish was running. I reached across Michael and flipped off the clicker and the sound of the stripping monofilament was sweeter and more natural. I turned to Ulis and clenched a fist and that old Bahamian face broke open and smiled.

I put my hand on Michael's tense shoulder and told him that he'd hooked him good and that he was a very, very good fish. Then I strapped the harness up onto the reel and got him comfortable and adjusted the chair so that his legs were slightly flexed and he could use them to push. Ulis slowed the engines to idle and threw them out of gear and some of the rod pressure eased. The boat stopped moving forward and everything Michael felt was the fish.

"Better get that outrigger in," Ulis shouted down.

I turned to it, but Ciro was already there pulling the halyard down. He loosed the line from the clip and cranked it up to the leader. Then he looked at Michael in the chair, holding the bent over rod and smiled at me, but it was a cautious smile. That bridge rod had a 9/0 reel, an old Senator that was my favorite for school tuna and marlin of average size, but nobody's first choice for anything big.

I said to Ciro, "The drag's set loose and there's plenty of line on the spool."

He nodded, bent over and flipped the bait in the boat.

Michael held the rod. "He's still running."

"He will for some time yet. Just keep that tip up and try to relax for now."

"He's taking a lot of line," Michael said.

"That's all right. The more he has, the more he has to drag through the water."

Michael watched the line going out. The rod tip went sideways a bit and I reached under the chair and loosened the lock at the base so the chair could swivel.

"Want to do this?" I asked Ciro.

"Sure."

"Just turn him enough to keep him lined up with the fish."

He stood behind his son and took hold of the chairback. I climbed up the ladder and looked at Ulis.

"It's a big fish," I said.

"I know it." He put the clutches in gear to get some steerage. He turned the wheel slightly to reposition the boat and threw the clutches out again.

"As soon as he stops, I'll get Mike pumping and we can back down on him. Let's try to whip him fast."

Ulis nodded. "He had to hit on that little fucking reel."

"I should have thought of that when I rigged it with the biggest bait we had."

"I watched you do it."

"It can hold him if we do everything smooth. What weight's that line?"

"Eighty pound. First hundred yard double with a Bimini Twist."

"I hate to think of a knot anywhere on that spool."

"Ain't no other way to double that line, Mon."

"If I had time I would've bought a thousand yards of dacron and spliced it on all the reels right."

"You coulda done it last night, but you were too busy skinnin' your knees."

"What would you know about that?"

"Bones was in Five Dogs, saw the whole damn thing. I didn't figure it was you until a little while ago."

"He didn't know either?"

"Naw, said it was just some white guy off a boat. Bones run off when the police get there. Long story about that."

"Tell me after we get this fish."

"Quick as we can, fightin' man."

I climbed down and stood next to Michael. More than half the reel was stripped and line was still running out and not much slower.

Michael turned to me. "Should we tighten the drag?"

"Not until you're down to the spool. That fish is still strong. I've seen rods break and fish lost because somebody hit the drag too soon. Let him run, Mike. It's what he's supposed to be doing."

I felt the sun strong on my neck and went to the wheelhouse and found Ciro and Michael's caps and gave them to them.

"Where's yours?" asked Ciro.

"I can't think with a hat on. Are you comfortable, Mike?"

"Yeah."

"Let me know if that harness or anything needs to be adjusted."

The fish had taken another hundred yards. He'd be a long way out when he finally stopped, but we could use the boat to get him.

"I wish he'd jump," I said out loud.

"I'd love to see him," said Michael.

"So would I. When a billfish jumps early in the run he fills the little sacs along his underside with air and he can't go very deep after that. Young fish jump early but this hombre's too smart."

I looked around us again. Andros wasn't in sight nor was the weedline or any boats. Then the reel slowed and stopped and turned again slowly and stopped.

"Reel," I said to Michael.

He yanked back on the rod and wound down, barely getting a turn.

"Easy, easy," I said. "Pump all the way and reel down slow just like you did with that dolphin. Don't try to get much, just get it steady."

Michael calmed down and worked the fish, getting used to the motion and better at it, using not just his arms and back, but his legs against the foot rest of the chair.

"That's it, get a rhythm going. Rest when you need to, just sit with that rod tip up and start to reel again when you feel like it."

I turned up to Ulis. "Throw her in reverse."

I felt the revolutions speed slightly as we went out of gear and then slow again and the pitch of reverse that was unnatural in the open sea. We idled back in the direction of the line and Michael was reeling faster. He got about a hundred yards in and his hands were sweaty and starting to slip on the cranking handle so I asked Ciro to find two pairs of the white cotton work gloves below. He brought them out and I stuffed a pair in my back pocket. When the line was at an angle too sharp to keep backing on, Ulis took the boat out of gear again. Michael brought each hand free from the rod and I slipped a glove on, one then the other. He rested a half-minute and tried to work the fish closer. He brought in about ten inches of line on each pump. He got twenty more feet on the fish when the rod bent double like the first running strike and line began peeling off.

Michael cursed, watching the line he'd worked so hard for disappearing.

"It's his second run, Mike. He's strong yet. Let him tire himself out." Then I turned, went to the ladder and climbed half-way up.

"So much for beating him quick," I said to Ulis.

He nodded. "He runnin' like he don't know he's hooked."

I climbed back down and Michael looked up at me. I couldn't see his eyes behind his sunglasses. The line ran steadily out, just as fast.

"How are you doing?" I asked him.

"All right."

I knew what he was thinking and said, "That line'll come in easier the second time."

"He'll be twice as tired as the first time," Ciro said from behind us.

"He wasn't tired the first time," Michael said, but he grinned a little.

I squeezed his shoulder." "He saw the boat. He doesn't know what we are, just that we have hold of him."

The fish ran steadily in the same direction, which was north-west, down to the last quarter of line on the reel. He stopped at once, possibly no longer seeing us nor sensing the vibrations we made and, thinking he'd run clear, swam slowly sideways, testing the bounds of his new tether.

I signaled to Ulis to go into reverse and we backed down again. Ulis used a little throttle this time and small seas slapped the flat of the transom as we went back awkwardly, the sounds of the engines alternately audible and muffled as the exhausts bobbed under and up. Michael was getting line in fast.

"My right hand's like a claw," he said.

"Try not to stop now, Mike." I knew that feeling, more like a cramp than fatigue. Mike had enough of Ciro in his back and arms, but almost nobody had the hands for a really good fish.

Again the line went vertical and Ulis threw the boat out of gear then ahead a touch to stop the momentum and back to neutral. We idled, rocking gently and Michael worked the fish.

Ulis waved me up. I climbed the ladder and he pointed to a temperature gauge.

"Starboard engine's hot," he said.

"Aw, shit."

The needle was close to one-ninety. About one-sixty was normal.

"Take her, I'll have a look."

I didn't need to move us. We stayed pointed southeast. Down in the cockpit Ciro swiveled the chair slightly and tightened it. Michael worked slowly, not at all bad, really, for an out of shape college kid with a day's experience. I watched the bend of the rod tip flex deeper with his pulling stroke, deepest at the top and then flatten as he reeled down. I watched the rod and the tightly stretched monofilament that was double-lined above the transom and at an angle to it and eighty or ninety feet below in the clear, incredibly deep blue behind the boat, I saw something green several times like the stroke of a fan.

In the middle of a back haul the rod bent double and line began paying out.

"I saw him, Mike," I said quickly and leaned over the bridge rail. "He's running from the boat."

Ciro looked up at me. "You see him now?"

"No, but I saw him turn a second ago. Let him pull himself out."

The starboard engine stopped running then and Ulis came from below and stood in the cockpit and looked at Michael and the line running back out. He climbed up and I gave him the wheel.

"There's a leak in the heat exchanger."

"Big?"

"Big enough to start the bilge pump runnin," he said and looked down at Michael.

"Fish is green yet."

I nodded and climbed down and stood next to Michael. He was sweat-soaked through his T-shirt and was glad to see me, but he didn't smile.

"Do you feel all right?"

He nodded, looking at the line.

"He's big as a horse."

"Really?" He said it slowly, eyes on the reel. Half the line was back out.

"Has to be to be able to see him that deep. You're doing beautiful with him."

He shook his head, watching the reel turn.

"Let him run himself ragged with all that line. Let him hang himself on it."

Ciro massaged his shoulders.

"One more time and we'll whip him."

He grinned then, bravely at me and I half-climbed the ladder to the bridge.

"Got any Marine-Tex or anything to plug that water leak," I asked Ulis.

"No, damn it."

"Well, we need that engine when the fish stops."

"I don't want to blow a piston, Mon."

"You won't. A diesel can run a little hot. I saw a six-seventy-one in a dragger come in so overheated that the paint burned off her valve covers and started a fire in the bilge. Water pump went. Guy fixed her and changed oil and ran the next day?"

"No shit?"

I shook my head. "We can use her when we need her, just watch your gauge. Let's back down on this son of a bitch and get a gaff in him."

The fish stayed deep. He ran and stopped and ran again and then Michael turned him and started him coming. Ulis fired the bad engine and threw the boat in reverse.

I whirled my arm above my head.

"Turn 'em up," I shouted.

The engines grew louder and, barefoot on the deck, I felt the hull vibrate. The props weren't made to turn in that direction very fast and they twisted water back over the shafts like corkscrews.

The rod eased and I told Michael to get in line as fast as he could. It came easier, he didn't have to pump, and I stayed next to him, making sure he guided it in evenly over the reel with his thumb. We backed fast several minutes, swells slapping the transom and throwing up spray. Then the line got steep and I yelled to Ulis to take us out of gear. We had three quarters of the line back and Michael was exhausted.

"Good," I told him, rubbing his shoulders. "Rest now a minute and we'll bring him the rest of the way."

Then the line moved in a different way, flattening out again, but with less weight and I knew the fish was coming up.

"Reel now, Mike. He's on top and most of the line's still deep."

He grimaced and brought it in, perhaps thirty more yards and, far out beyond the stern, the marlin flew, shaking his head, and landed with an enormous splash.

Ciro and Ulis hollered.

"It's him," Michael cried.

"It sure is, buddy. Get line in."

The fish jumped again, high and closer, clear of the water and glaring at us. We saw him a long moment and everything he was with the long, ridged dorsal above his huge head like the crown of a savage king.

"Mother of God," said Ciro.

I watched his tail fly up and follow him in. I'd never seen a bigger fish.

"Turn him a little, Ciro," I said and looked up at Ulis who grinned and shook his head.

Line rolled out and Michael rested, holding the rod. It was the fish's last run.

"He won't go deep now, Michael. He'll quit in a minute and then bring him in steady. We can't back on him, he's too close and we don't want him under the boat. Just work him like you have been and we'll get him soon."

"Christ, I hope so," he said, but he was excited and stronger now that he'd seen the fish.

I shouted up to Ulis.

"How's that engine?"

"Heating up."

The fish took another fifty yards, but he was weaker and only about thirty feet deep. He stopped and Michael worked him slowly, beautifully. He'd get ten yards and the fishwould turn and run and stop and he'd get ten more and then twenty and then the fish was only thirty yards behind the boat and I knew Ulis could see him.

"Fifteen yards to that leader, Michael."

"You sure?" he asked, sucking air.

"I'm sure, old bud."

"Oh, man," he sighed.

He groaned again, but it was like a weight lifter straining the last ones out, knowing it would be over soon.

Then down below us something silver grew in the dark blue like the coming of a star.

"I can see him, Mike," I said.

The rod pumped up and down twice next to me, but no line came in.

"Ten more yards, Michael. Bring him in."

"I can't, he said.

"Sure you can." Nice and easy."

"I can't turn the reel. It's stuck."

"What?" I spun, thinking he'd let too much line build up in one place and jammed it, but I looked at the reel and the line was fairly flat and even.

"Hold the rod," I said, knowing for me to touch the reel in any way was against tournament rules, but this was repair to equipment. I carefully loosened the drag and nothing happened, no line ran out. I looked up at Ulis.

"It's frozen. The fucking spool must have spread."

Ulis bit his lower lip and shook his head. He looked quickly behind the boat where the marlin flashed like a sword.

"Handline 'im in," he yelled down to me.

I shook my head. It was against I.G.F.A. rules.

"I can't touch that line. It'll disqualify him."

Ciro spoke up. "What if Michael does it?"

"You can't handline a fish until you reach the leader."

I looked at Michael who held the rod, watching the tip bow and quiver, feeling each of the fish's movements direct, now that there was no belly of line in the water between them.

I put a hand on Michael's shoulder. "Here's what we have to do, Mike. We have to get you out of the chair and back you up into the wheelhouse with that rod until I can reach the leader."

"Shit, Jim."

"We can't touch the line or the rod. We aren't supposed to touch you either, but fuck that, we'll guide you back as far as we can and steady you."

"Oh, man," he said.

"Will you try that, Michael?"

He nodded and I raised up the foot rest and slid it forward and out of the chair. I laid it along the starboard side of the cockpit and then Ciro and I unhooked the harness from the chair. I found the gimbal with the rod holder and strapped it around Michael and helped him get the rod butt out of the chair and into it. I looked up at Ulis who was gently easing the boat forward. If the fish swam under the boat at that shallow depth, the line could hit the props. Ciro and I slid Michael forward and held him on either side by the upper arms. We sidestepped him away from the chair and shuffled him backwards. It was awkward.

"Crouch," I said to Michael. "Bend your knees."

He did and was more stable, but the weight of the fish was terrific. Once or twice, both of his feet were completely off the deck in the middle of a step and it was only Ciro and me keeping him up.

The three of us reached the wheelhouse and Michael had to lean the rod tip forward to make it under. We stopped him and Ciro got behind him and held him tight around the waist.

"Let go of that rod if you go overboard," I said.

"I won't go overboard."

They wedged themselves against the table that ran along the inside of the wheelhouse. I left them and ran to the stern. I saw the leader a foot under water and the huge shape of the fish below it. I reached, but the line was still too far out diagonally.

"Take her out of gear," I shouted up to Ulis.

"She already out," he shouted back.

I looked at Michael and Ciro.

"I still can't reach it. Move back another two feet."

I watched them struggle and gradually the swivel drifted nearer the surface. I drove my thighs tight to the stern, bent as far as I could keep my balance and reached passed the monofilament, into the water and got my hand on the swivel.

I felt the fish then, more than an impossible weight. It was as if through that leader ran the current from a firestorm at the center of the earth. He swam in a half-circle fifteen feet from the boat, slowly whipping his head to shake the thing that held him. He was deep blue and shining, slashing his bill against the wire, trying to kink and break it.

I hauled and brought the swivel up and got my left hand on the wire, finally taking some of the pressure off Michael. The fish was another foot closer, moving and flashing in the blue like a dream. Wedged in the stern, I strained and brought him up another foot. I struggled to hold him, cursing his anger and his wild fighting heart.

"Jesus Christ."

It was Ciro's voice somewhere behind me along the gunwale.

Ulis yelled excitedly from the bridge.

"He gonna throw that hook, Mon!"

"I can't move him," I yelled into the water.

"Get him in," shouted Ulis.

"HE'S TOO GREEN," I screamed.

"Hold him there," yelled Ulis.

"That's what the hell I'm trying to do!"

Without trying to turn my head I yelled, "Rest, Mike, but keep that rod tip up if I can't hold him. If he pulls you forward just come forward, I won't let him pull you over."

And then to Ciro.

"Get the gaff up and ready. Make sure the line's clear. When I get him up, ease the gaff down under him and set it in him and keep raising 'till the hook breaks loose."

The fish stopped whipping his head. He switched his tail and turned around and swam the half-circle in the other direction. I couldn't bring him up just yet, but he couldn't go down again either. We pulled against each other and I heard Ulis' voice.

"Get him up, Mon."

"Not just yet," I said, still looking down.

Michael said, "Tell me what he looks like."

Ciro answered him. "He's unbelievable, Mike. He's really long and blue."

The fish swam against the wire.

"He's still strong," I said to Ciro.

"Is there anything I can do to help you?"

"Just stay ready with that gaff."

"Will he quit, ever?"

"No. Never. But he'll get weak."

"Can you hold him, Jim?"

"I have to." We were up against the wall. There was no give except my arms.

Michael asked, "Can the two of you horse him in."

"Not with this wire. I'm too worried about how he's hooked to try that."

Ciro said to me, "Ulis says he's hooked good."

"He was. The hook could be straightening out by now." As soon as it was out I regretted saying it. Michael had enough to worry about.

Thirty more seconds past. I was feeling it in my back and I bent my knees a bit further which helped. I watched the tautness of the wire and the angle it made in the light below the surface. It disappeared after a few feet, the only thing that held us to the fish.

"Stay in that wheelhouse, Mike."

I decided to try a little then, to see if he would come.
I brought both fists a few inches closer to my chest.

"I need your help now," I said to Ciro. "Come behind me and get a good hold on my belt."

"Right"

I felt both his fistholds in my belt. I crouched a little more, wedging myself tighter in the stern.

"Let's try it," I said, but not very loud, as though the fish could hear me. I held with my left and brought my right six inches under it and took a loop of wire. The fish was still strong, but he came an inch or so. That was fine, I'd take him in inches if I could last that long.

The line gathered in the cockpit, I told Ciro to pull it close to him and to heap it spread out and clear of everything.

I got six feet on the marlin, fist to chest. From behind me Ciro watched him come, Michael was still in the wheelhouse. The angle might have been too steep for Ulis to see from the bridge, but I could see him. He was nine feet below me and as brightly colored as if electrified. I saw the shank of the hook way up in the top half of his mouth. He fluttered his gills every few moments and in the clear water I saw his bill, longer and thicker than a baseball bat.

In the middle of a pull, I was using my back now, the fish whipped his head and nearly took my arms from their sockets. I couldn't hold him.

"HOLD ON, MIKE," I screamed.

The leader bit through the cotton of the gloves, I barely opened my fist in time. The heaped-up line shot out and over me, went tight and down and hit my shoulder like a bull whip.

Michael yelled and stumbled forward. I heard him hit the deck and I waited for the rod to fly up and take my head off.

"GODDAMN FUCKING MONSTER!" Ulis screamed from the bridge.

Ciro had let go of me to try to get to Michael. I held to the gunwale with both hands and locked my knees against the cover-ing board. I couldn't have gotten out from under the line if I wanted to. With Michael lying on his side on the deck and still holding the frozen rod, my back was about the only thing that could give. I felt line dig into me and stretch tight.

I yelled to Ciro, "Is he all right?"

"Yeah," I heard Michael say, obviously hurt.

"Can you get him to his feet?"

"I don't know," Ciro said in a father's voice. "I'll try."

Ulis yelled down, "I'm gonna come down and cut that line."

"NO!" Michael shouted.

I was proud of him, he wouldn't quit the fish.

I yelled to Ulis, "Stay up there and keep the boat straight. I don't want this line around my neck."

The pressure on my back would have been bad enough with half-inch manilla. The sharpness of the line was like a scissor. Then the angle of pain changed and I knew Michael had gotten to his feet.

"Walk back, old buddy," I said. "Just like you did before."

Ciro struggled with him and the line started to creep back over my shoulder, cutting in.

I grimaced and said, "Please try to keep that rod tip up, Michael."

He understood why and said, "I'm sorry, Jim."

"That's all right. You're the best guy in the world for holding on to that rod."

He said, "I'll try to keep the pressure off you." He was close to tears. It was his day to learn what a big fish could do to a man.

The wire came back up and quivered. The fish was down in the shadow beneath the boat, but I could see him. I got a hand below the swivel and asked Ciro to help me as soon as the pressure was off Mike.

I started on the leader for the second time, hand under hand, hold with one, make a loop with the other. Ciro had me by the belt and I brought the fish slowly. The last try had taken all he had, but he still swam against the leader. I felt the same way about him, but was rougher with him and brought him faster. I'd seen the hook in tight and my arms and shoulders were about gone. I stopped a few seconds to spell myself. The fish hung ten feet below us.

"Let go of me and get the flying gaff ready."

Ciro took it from where it lay on the deck and held it with the nylon line along the haft and in both fists.

"Where do you want me?" he asked quickly.

"On my left when I move over. When I have him up, just ease that hook under him and raise up like you're lifting him."

"All right." He was nervous but I thought he could do it.

"Want me to come down," Ulis asked from the bridge.

"No, Cap, stay where you are in case I can't hold him. Ciro, is that gaff line fast to the cleat?"

"Yes."

I took a good wrap of wire around my glove and hauled smooth. I took another wrap and sidestepped a few inches at a time to let Ciro in the corner. I brought the fish another foot and the boat actually listed with the strength and weight of him. I was taking everything in my shoulders, my arms, and my wrists.

The fish was seven feet below us and we saw him as well as if he were out of the water, his dorsal and pectoral fins, which seemed black but were really dark blue, the bright blue of his head and back and the thin blue vertical stripes along the white shine of his sides. I spelled myself again and we looked at him.

"My God," Ciro said.

Mike had moved up to the gunwale, still holding the rod. I saw him out of the corner of my eye. He looked over the side at the fish, afraid to say a word.

I shouted up to Ulis.

"Is anybody standing on the gaff line?"

"No," he said quickly. "It's clear."

"Get ready, Ciro."

He'd been holding the gaff at port arms like a rifle and now he held the hook over the water. I brought the fish three more feet, watching the V-wake the leader made in the current. Ciro started the gaff down.

"Not yet."

"No? Okay."

I took a double wrap of wire around my glove. If I lost any fingers now it would mean we lost the fish and I wouldn't give a damn. I hauled up, arching my back and got another double wrap with the other glove.

"Try to get it under him now, Ciro."

He did it quick and beautifully, leaning forward just enough not to lose his balance and dipped the hook under the fish. He took another hand hold farther down the shaft and raised the gaff higher, grunting, but the hook didn't break from the handle.

"Hold him. Hold him," I said. "I'll help you."

Even though completely exhausted, the fish felt the gaff. His eye grew large and he tossed his huge head. I still held a handful of double wrapped leader wire and almost went overboard. I banged both legs on the side of the cockpit, recovered and tried to get my hands free. I fumbled and the fish tossed again and my hand tore away from me toward the water.

"Mike, get me the wire cutter."

He dropped the rod on the deck and went someplace behind me. Ciro still fought with the gaff and then two black hands appeared in front of me. They were strong and gnarled as old mahogany and they held the wire without gloves, giving me slack.

"Get yer hand loose," said Ulis from beside me.

Water flew in front of us. The marlin broke the surface with his tossing. Ciro choked up on the gaff and I got an inch or so of slack. I yanked my hand from the glove which stayed wrapped in the wire, whipping tight between us and the fish like a party streamer. When I knew I was loose, I turned to help Ciro, but Ulis was already there. They hauled together and there was another explosion of seawater that soaked everybody and the hook finally broke free. The fish swam out a few feet with the hook in him and the gaff line holding the hook. The leader was strung parallel with the half-inch nylon, the glove still caught and touching the water. We had him.

"YES, GODDAMN IT!" I hollered and hugged Ulis and Ciro and we spun and got hold of Michael, pounding him and whooping and the four of us danced around the cockpit, skipping over the rod and the wrecked reel.

"WE DID IT! WE DID IT!" Michael was yelling.

"You did it," I told him. "And you did everything right."

"I was afraid the whole time. I was afraid to say a word that we'd lose him." He was watery-eyed so I grabbed the bucket, filled it half-full over the side and hit him with it. Then I hit Ciro. Then Ulis.

"Easy, easy, we ain't got him in the boat yet," Ulis said, his wide strong face full of teeth. He shut down the bad engine.

"He ain't goin' nowhere, Cap," I said. "I'll rig a tailrope around him if you'll find me some line."

The gaff had finished the marlin. He struggled with something, stopped moving and glared at us. There had never been fear in his eye, only rage now going dim. The line held him hooked and stretched alongside the boat and we looked at his length and girth and the tremendous heft of his bill.

I said to Michael, "Better get your camera before his color starts to fade."

Ulis handed me a coil of half-inch nylon and I doubled four feet of it, tied it off and brought it inside itself. Ciro and I pulled in the gaffline and brought the fish next to the boat. We took a few turns around a stern cleat and held him there. I opened the loop of line, bent over the side and worked it over the enormous tail. It had to be four and a half feet.

"He got half a moon for a tail," Ulis said.

"Wide as an eagle," I said, pulling the loop tight.

Michael had been on the bridge taking pictures. He brought the camera down.

"How do we ever get him in the boat?"

"That's what the ginpole's for," I said, motioning to the heavy, five-inch square wood shaft that looked like a stubby mast. It ran from the deck up passed the end of the wheelhouse and four feet above the deck of the bridge. For the first time Michael noticed it and the small pulleys at the top and bottom.

Ulis untied and unwrapped the extra line that held the block and fall tight to the ginpole. He unhooked the bottom pulley, slacked the line and worked it out about five feet. Then he set it over the side.

"Hook him up," he said.

I asked Ciro to uncleat the gaff line and, with both my hands on the bill, led the big fish slowly ahead until his tail and the tailrope were even with the pulley trailing inthe water. I made a sheetbend of the tailrope and hooked the pulley hook and nodded to Ulis.

Ulis dropped the line to the deck and looked at Michael.

"Ain't my fish, Mon."

Michael handed him the camera and picked up the line.

"What do I do?"

"Pull down in steady strokes," I said.

And he did, laboring in the sun, feeling not the fighting weight of the fish, but the actual weight that was no less impressive. It was a light tackle and a hard pull. The tail came out of the water six inches at a time and the boat listed greater the higher he came.

Quietly, Ulis asked me, "What do you think he is?"

"I'm afraid to guess. Three-fifty at least."

"He better than four. I know it."

"He might be the one. Not that I care, but wouldn't it be something for the kid to win the tournament?"

"For his first fish, dead on."

Michael stopped to rest.

"Take some pictures of him coming up, Dad."

When the marlin was halfway, I worked the gaff hook out. Out of the water he was thicker and more powerful looking. His mouth was open and he had the same angry look in his eye that he died with.

We ran the pulley as high as it would go, but few ginpoles were built for a fish that big and most of the head hung in the water. I rigged some of the nylon around the base of the marlin's bill and Ciro and Michael and I pulled astern then up and got the huge head over the gunwale and into the cockpit. We stood looking at him in the sunlight.

Untying the line from the bill, I said to Michael, "He's fought other marlin and quite a few sharks with this thing."

"He'd fight sharks?"

"You bet. He'd kill a mako if there was only one of 'em."

"That would be something to see."

I pointed to a long scar on his side.

"That's where another male slashed him."

"Whoa. Think he messed him up?"

"Probably did a job on him."

"I still don't believe we have him, Jim."

"He's really something, isn't he? Tell me how you feel."

"Like I'm in shock. Every muscle seems strange and light and I can hardly close my hands."

"Tomorrow you'll feel like you wrestled him."

"I don't care what I'll feel like."

I grinned. "I know you don't."

Ciro looked at me and then Ulis.

"I don't suppose we have a blue marlin flag on board?"

Ulis smiled and went below. For a moment I thought he'd take revenge and steal something blue from my bag, but what he came up with looked like the first blue marlin flag ever made. It was a strange sort of material and so frayed that most of the marlin's bill was gone and it looked more like a tuna. The rest of the flag was faded and covered with rust stains.

Ulis held it up with pride. Ciro and I started up.

"That thing belongs in a museum."

"When was the last time you had it out?"

Ulis tied it to the halyard and ran it up the outrigger.

"Impressive," said Ciro. "Like our engine and no radio."

Michael and I let the pulley back down and the fish lay the length of the cockpit. We covered most of him in clean rags and wet them down in seawater. We weren't trying to preserve anything for a taxidermist, he was too big to mount, but it seemed important to keep the sun off him. We worked the big Mustad hook from his mouth. It had changed shape slightly but not much. I cut it from the wire and gave it to Michael. I stripped the baits from the other leaders, tossed them overboard, coiled the leaders, and hung them under the fighting chair. I felt our good engine turning up and Ulis swung us around.

Ciro had a bottle of rum out.

"Bar's open," he said.

"Let's all have one," I said.

The boat was slow with one engine and ran with the port side low with the weight of the fish. We climbed the ladder, handed Ulis a rum and fought the fish again, slapping each other, waving and gesturing, pouring ice down Michael's shirt, and holding down Ulis and threatening to strip him and fly his underwear. We were all the way passed Andros when we finally settled down. We stayed on the bridge, the four of us, the long run across the unbelievably deep channel to The Great Bank where Little Cay rose in the sun.

Ulis started the bad engine to use through the inlet and I brought the outriggers back up. It was almost four, but we were the only boat coming in. Most of the fleet was up around Northwest Light which wasn't that far and way off in that direction we could see about a dozen white hulls scattered over a mile or so near what was probably the light buoy. They trolled back and forth and would until dark.

We came through the rocks and kids fishing on the jetty saw the marlin flag and, on higher rocks, the kids could see the fish in the cockpit and they started yelling and pointing and quite a few of them reeled in their lines when we slowed down and passed them. They grouped up and started across the jetty, following us in to see the fish weighed.

We idled past the gas dock and our slip to the clubhouse where a few boats had been in with fish already. I climbed up along the wheelhouse to the bow. The group of people at the scales saw our flag, the tide was out and we were low in the water, and they saw the fish easily as we came up and they started to speak amongst themselves and to look at the fish.

We came alongside the bulkhead and the dockmaster, who was one of the judges, and two island kids threw us lines. I secured the bow and was making the springline fast to the midships cleat when I saw Sonny standing above me on the dock. He was barefoot and in khaki shorts and a khaki shirt that had *The Katherine's* name stitched in blue above a breast pocket. He stood half-smiling with his hands on his hips.

"Get into one?" he asked in that whiskey and water rasp.

"Yep," I said, taking a turn around the cleat. The trick was not to look at him. "You?"

"Raised one and lost him. Hutch had to fly out so we came in early."

"Oh." I knew he was looking at the fish.

"Jump, did he?" He was all teeth out of the corner of my eye. I pushed my lips together, undid the line and retied it.

"He gave us a little show."

"Any size?" I heard that rasp break when he said "size."

"Keeper, I guess." I couldn't stifle the grin any longer.

"Keeper," he demanded. "He's a goddamn horse!"

I climbed up on the dock and we grappled with each other. I nearly fell in and he steadied me and pulled me around him and we walked to where a crowd had gathered looking down into the boat.

Using the fall pulley as a guyline, the dockboys swung the boom of the hoist across the dock and over the cockpit. Ulis caught the pulley block and hooked it to the marlin's tailrope. The dockboys took up the slack and hauled on the line and we saw the width of the marlin's tail above the gunwale and then the rest of him came, stage by stage, as they drew the line. The last seven pulls brought his head up. The tip of his bill made a black scrape along the teak before it went vertical. Once he was clear, the boat stopped listing as well as if three men had jumped off.

They raised him higher and swung him over the dock. There was no difference in the faces of the crowd, judges, boat owners, crews, locals in from town and marina help. Even the smallest of the Bahamian kids in shorts knew what they were looking at. Now, like a religious image, the seldom-seen creature of a hundred stories hung for them in splendor. They loved and were frightened by the great animal and looked at it without making a sound.

Sonny was quiet, too. He twisted his head scientifically. "What'll he go?" I asked him.

"Four at least, four and a quarter. I've only seen one bigger."

Two of the judges turned him, hooking the tail line to the scale and easing off the pulley and we saw the old two foot scar on his underside. They brought a stepladder and the dockmaster climbed up and adjusted the weights and waited for them to balance. The crowd was quiet except for the kids.

The dockmaster studied the weights.

"Four hundred seventy-one pounds," he said sharply.

There were whistles and cheers. Sonny slapped me and I pointed down in the cockpit to the rod and broken reel.

Michael and Ciro were talking to the judges and a Bahamian in a white short-sleeved shirt and green trousers walked up.

"Excuse me," he said. He extended his hand and I shook it.

"Congratulations on your fish. We would like to know if you would be interested in donating it to the Nassau Orphanage?"

"I'm pretty sure we would, but you'll have to ask that gentlemen over there. It's his fish."

"Certainly," he said. We shook hands again and he headed for Michael. Sonny followed him to get a closer look at the marlin.

"Nice catch, handsome." Inez had drifted up through the crowd and stood next to me.

"Thanks," I said. She wore sunglasses and was grinning.

"Was he wonderful?"

"He was. I wish you could have seen him."

"So do I, brother. Were you wonderful, too?"

"I was all right. I was just the hired hand."

"I'll bet you were just fine. I'll bet you were magnificent."

I looked at her forehead, at her hair pulled back, and at that smile.

"You better get out of here before I kiss you in front of all these people."

"Like this?" She grabbed me by the ears and kissed me sharply on the cheek.

"That wasn't exactly what I had in mind."

"Will it do, brother?"

"I guess it'll have to."

Ciro yelled to me.

"Come on. They want to take pictures."

I excused myself and went over and stood with them.

Ciro said, "Three other boats have fish but no size estimates are in yet. It looks like us so far."

I nodded and looked at the crowd while the photographers fiddled with their stuff. Then I turned to Ulis.

"Didn't do too bad, did we, Cap?"

"Best fish ever," he said. "Best crew ever."

We shook hands and he looked at me.

"You got heart, Mon. And you know how to fish."

"And you can run a boat."

"And you can rig bait."

"So could you."

"And squid now."

"And squid now."

When the photographers finished, Ulis started *The Tina*. With two dockboys to help with the lines, he brought her back to the slip. Ciro had Michael and I stand around for more pictures. He went to the commissary and bought another roll of film and shot it then he walked off in the direction of the marina office.

The crowd began to move, people turning their heads and stepping from the center of the dock to the sides. A moment later I saw the pickup coming through, backing toward us, driven by the same guy who had picked us up the first afternoon. He stopped near the marlin.

"Raise any hell?" he asked us, grinning.

"Some," I said. "Raised a hell of a fish."

"He is a hell of a fish," he said, getting out. They swung the arm of the scale and used the pulleys to lower the fish to the bed of the truck. The springs squeaked and the tires bulged and the head of the marlin lay on the tailgate.

Michael stroked his head and the broad part of his bill.

"I'll never bring another one in," he said quietly. "I'll release every other one."

"Of course." I said.

"I don't like seeing him dead like this, but I don't feel bad about it."

"You shouldn't. He was going to die someday just like you and I will and we never would have seen him. He gave us that."

"All I wanted to do was to catch him. And then I didn't want it to be over. It was the most wonderful thing being connected to him like that."

"It was everything he had, Mike."

"Yes. And now I know why you do it. It's like nothing else matters."

"Everything still does. He'll only make it matter more."

"You don't lose it, do you?" he asked suddenly. "The way he is, I mean. You don't lose that do you, Jim?"

And I knew now that you didn't.

"It'll always be right there where you need it, Mike. Whatever happens after today."

"Three days ago I wouldn't have known that."

"I wouldn't have either."

Ciro walked up. In his thick hands were four plastic bar glasses half-filled with dark rum.

"Time the crew drank a toast. Where's Ulis?"

"Back at the boat," I said.

"We'll have another one later," Ciro said, handing us each a cup. We touched them together and sipped it down. The rum was smooth and warm as the late sun. The pickup started and Michael followed it down the dock to the metal cutting tables. They'd steak out the marlin and ice it down for the kids in Nassau and Michael could get the bill shipped to a taxidermist on the mainland.

Ciro knocked back the extra rum and we walked slowly to the slip. Ulis was down in the bilge. He'd borrowed some lead putty and was smearing it over the leak. I asked him if he needed help.

"No, it's on. Need to let it set up half an hour before she can run."

"Are you going to fuel up?"

Ulis nodded.

"We'll come back and settle up." I tapped Ciro. "Let's take a look around."

Ciro and I walked the length of the marina. People on several of the tournament boats waved to us as we passed. We came to *The Katherine* and everyone was on board except Hutchinson. Inez sat on the bridge, leaning on the control panel, having a drink with Barry and a youngish man and woman. Sonny was down in the cockpit standing near Mrs. H.who sat in the fighting chair. An elderly couple in the boat alongside leaned on the gunwale chatting with her.

Inez saw us first. She still wore sunglasses and she smiled. She cheered and started to clap and Barry and the others followed until everyone on the boat and the other boat was clapping, I waved and heard Mrs. Hutchinson's husky voice shout "Bravo."

I looked at Inez. There was something of that day in the lighthouse I wouldn't give up, but the old thought had outlived itself. Getting it back wouldn't have been enough, anyhow. That time had finished and I was ready to make something else.

I waved again to all of them, knowing it was goodbye, the weight of it finally off and I realized I was smiling, really smiling.

"Well," Ciro said, walking, "what do you think, partner?"

"I think things'll be all right from here on in."

"Sure," he shrugged. "Why shouldn't they be?"

We took a few more steps and I said, "And I think you have good reason to be proud of your son."

"Thanks. So do I. And we think you're a hell of a fisher-man."

"I'd say you're both right for once."

He slugged me on the arm and we passed the commissary and the restaurant and the weighing area where the fish had hung and still a crowd milled, waiting for other boats. We met Michael at the cleaning tables. He walked up grinning and holding the huge bill in both hands. It was black now, but would come back to him mounted the same dark blue it had been when he'd first seen it. Ciro and I passed it back and forth, hefting its amazing weight and balance, thrusting it and whipping it side to side a few times like the weapon it was. Then we gave it back to Michael. He set the heavy end on his shoulder, holding it near the tip and the three of us walked the rest of the way to the gas dock where Ulis fueled *The Tina.*

We helped him finish up and set the last of our gear up on the dock. Ciro found the rum bottle and poured what was left into four coffee cups. We sat in the galley with the marlin's bill across the table and wrote Ulis a check.

"Well," Ulis said, running his hand up and down the bill, "did we win it?"

No one answered him. I watched his gnarled hand travel the length of the bill and I knew I was looking at his whole life.

It was Ciro who finally said, "We probably won."

Ulis nodded slowly and blinked.

"Good. That's everthin' then."

He finished his rum and shook hands with us all and Ciro promised to send him copies of the pictures. He started both engines and we cast him off and walked to the end of the dock as he glided the boat up alongside us, standing on the bridge.

He touched the throttles when he passed us and *The Tina* grew louder, digging into the current. She slipped away from us, throwing a little wake across the tiny harbor to the mouth of the inlet. When she was through the jetty Ulis turned and waved to us and touched the throttles again and she surged. She was running now, moving with the sea and Ulis swung the wheel, turning her for Nassau.

We waved but he didn't see us. We followed her around the rocks until all we could see was her tower lurching, the tournament flag and the blue marlin flag still flying in the wind.

Ciro put a hand on Michael's shoulder and mine and we started back up the dock. The breeze picked up, we heard it in the halyards and outriggers of the docked boats we passed. It was a sound that was sometimes lonely to me, but other times like the laughter of small children.

THE END